Letters From a

Bounty

Hunter

Jim Kennison (signature)

Jim Kennison

Outskirts Press, Inc.
Denver, Colorado

Letters From A Bounty Hunter
All Rights Reserved
Copyright © 2007 Jim Kennison
vr 1.0
Cover Image © 2007 JupiterImages Corporation
All Rights Reserved. Used With Permission.

Outskirts Press
http://www.outskirtspress.com

ISBN-10: 1-59800-952-4
ISBN-13: 978-1-59800-952-1

Outskirts Press and the "OP" logo are trademarks belonging to Outskirts Press, Inc.

Printed in the United States of America

Chapter 1

His throat was dry from the dust he'd been eating all day. The drive to Cheyenne took longer than anticipated. The winter snows had been heavy and the spring rains came just as the snow packs broke loose on the eastern slope of the Rockies. Even small creeks were impassable in places. Then came the constant, searing sun and the water was gone as fast as it had come.

The drive had started in the far north of Dakota Territory, lasting the better part of four months. Grass was scarce for the last fifty miles and part of the herd just lay down and died. The steers that did make it to the railhead looked like museum bone displays.

But it was over, and Jamison Jakes made his way toward the saloon and the cold beer that had been teasing his dreams for weeks. He needed a bath, but that could wait. The shave could wait. The change of clothes could wait. The beer had waited long enough. Having nothing but whiskey to unwind with since starting the drive, Jakes craved something cold.

He took a minute to slap his hat against his chaps and brush some of the dirt from the front and arms of his calico shirt. Seeing his reflection in the glass window of the hardware store, he stared curiously at the man looking back at him.

"My Lord," Jakes muttered half aloud. Then, more out of respect for the man inside the trail-worn leathery skin than the one he saw reflected in the window, he removed his bandanna, sopped it wet with water from a horse trough and rubbed it hard over his long, scraggly beard.

He stopped briefly before pushing through the saloon's swinging doors to watch the red August sun sink into a pool of purple clouds. Jakes was glad he'd decided to be a cowhand and was proud to be working in a part of the country where men are measured by their grit.

It was a good day in his life when he'd signed on as a wrangler for the Cheyenne Stock Growers Association. This new enterprise was in its fourth year of operation and had already contracted with most of the ranchers in western Dakota and eastern Montana to move their cattle to market. Jakes was thankful to have a steady job after years of drifting from place to place doing whatever work he could find.

There were just a handful of men in the barroom. Only a couple bothered to look up as Jakes took his place about half way down the long wooden bar.

"What'll it be?" asked the sad-faced bartender as he folded up the newspaper he'd been reading and swatted a fly edging its way toward a small pool of spilled whiskey on the counter.

"Big, cold mug of beer," replied Jamison Jakes rubbing his mouth with the back of his hand.

"I ain't got cold beer. If you want cold beer, come back in December and I'll give you cold beer."

"What the hell?" asked Jakes. "I thought Cheyenne was supposed to be a town with everything."

"Well, it just about is," replied the sad face. "We got gas

lamps that light up the night, we got boardwalks to keep the ladies' feet dry, we got a public privy with five holes so's there's no waitin', we got a jail with three cells, we got the cleanest whorehouse west of Omaha. And in the winter we got cold beer."

Jakes couldn't help but smile as he listened to the little man rattle on.

"Then I guess I'll have a warm beer."

"Got no warm beer. Nobody drinks warm beer!"

Jakes would have found the entire situation funny if he hadn't been so trail-weary.

"Then give me whiskey," Jakes said with resignation. "That is, if you got whiskey."

"Sure, I got whiskey. This here's a saloon ain't it?"

Sipping slowly on his drink, Jakes stared at the bottle in front of him. He suddenly realized that after drawing his pay and saying "solong" to the trail boss and the rest of the crew, with a promise he'd see them come next spring, he was once again alone. He was the only one of the crew staying around Cheyenne; the others had left quickly to return to their homes. Being alone wasn't new to Jakes and for the most part he preferred it that way. In his thirty-four years he'd never had a long-term friendship with anyone.

Halfway through his second glass of whiskey, he was aware of someone standing next to him.

"Howdy, mister. I wouldn't mind it one bit iffen you was to buy me a drink. No sir, not one bit."

Jamison Jakes slowly turned his head toward the youthful voice and looked into the face of a youngster who should've been more at home on a school yard than in a saloon.

"I don't think your ma would want you to be drinkin', son," Jakes said. "Especially hard liquor, and this place don't have nothin' but hard liquor."

"Mister, I been drinkin' long as I can remember. And my ma's so far away I'll never see her again anyways. Besides, you can't finish that whole bottle by yourself. Ain't right that a man should drink by hisself. No sir, just ain't right."

"Okay, son," Jamison Jakes replied, slapping the young man on the shoulder. "But, so help me, if your ma comes gunnin' for me, you're gonna be one sore-assed hombre."

"I do all the gunnin' in my family," said the youth.

The seriousness in his tone caught Jakes by surprise.

"You don't look all that mean," Jakes said lightly. "You gunned many men?"

"Ain't gunned none yet, but I intend to. I just ain't found the one who thinks he's the best. When I do, I'll give folks plenty to jaw about."

"Life's too short to go courtin' death," Jamison Jakes said somberly. "You better just get on to where you're stayin'."

Jakes finished his drink with one swallow and headed for the door. When he got there, he turned and looked back at the smooth-faced young man.

"When you're growin' up, life's pretty hard sometimes. But it can be even harder when you're grown. Don't be in such a hurry to be a man. There's more than enough time for that."

Chapter 2

Jamison Jakes was troubled some by the attitude of the boy he'd met in the saloon, but he was too tired to think about why. It was almost dark by the time he shuffled along the boardwalk toward the Hobson Hotel. The "Hot Bath" sign had caught his eye when he rode into town.

A short time later, in his room, Jakes sat in his grimy longjohns watching as the hotel maid poured steaming water into a large wooden bathtub. For the first time in weeks he felt relaxed. He lit the cheroot he'd carried since he left for the Dakota Territory, put his feet on the side of the tub, pulled his hat down over his eyes, and inhaled the sweet aroma of hot bath-oil steam.

"If you like, I can try to get them clothes clean by mornin', but I sure can't promise. Usually only charge two bits, but I ain't never tried to wash duds that dirty before."

"Just burn 'em," Jakes replied. "I'll give you two bits to take 'em out and burn 'em."

Within a few minutes, he settled deep in the tub, being careful to keep his cheroot dry. As he took off his hat and threw it across the room onto the bed, he thought again of the boy in the saloon.

What was it about that kid? He'd really liked the boy, he concluded, even though he was sassy and much too big for his britches. Why did he have that chip on his shoulder? What was he trying to prove? And why? Had Jakes known this boy before, or did the young man remind him of someone else? When he was looking at the boy, was it a young Jamison Jakes he saw?

Jakes had grown up quickly, the oldest of seven children born to Joshua Jakes and his wife Lucy. Joshua Jakes was a hard-working tenant farmer who raised tobacco in the rolling hills of central Kentucky. His wife, the former Lucy Jamison, had left a comfortable home in Boston to follow her husband to the frontier. She was a proud woman who carried herself tall and straight and set the table each night with the porcelain plates and shiny silverware she'd brought west.

Lucy Jamison Jakes was only seventeen when she bore her first child. He was christened Joshua Jamison Jakes but called Jamison so as not to be confused with his father. Lucy gave birth to six more children over the next nine years.

A tobacco farmer's life was a hard one. Very little money was made from a crop that took a year-round looking after. Jamison, along with his two brothers and four sisters, learned how to work early in life.

Each day of those early years taught Jakes the ethics of hard work and each evening was spent learning how to read and write and do numbers, as he and the other children would sit in front of the fireplace with Lucy Jakes. Lucy had completed ten years of schooling before getting married and enjoyed teaching her children

Being the oldest child was both good and bad for young Jamison. He was the first to hunt and fish so his father didn't have to leave his farm chores. And he soon discovered the consequences of disappointing others when he came home empty-handed.

Jamison Jakes decided early on that he didn't care for farming. Bringing in a good tobacco crop and seeing the look of satisfaction on his father's face was rewarding; but the thought of having to start over again, doing the same work year after year to create yet another crop, didn't interest him.

The Civil War provided the perfect opportunity for Jakes to leave farming behind. Although he was only sixteen when the war broke out, the promise of adventure, travel, and a uniform was more temptation than he could resist.

His leaving the farm was unceremonious at best, even cowardly, he was to think later. A note written in the middle of the night simply said he was off to the war, that he loved them all and that he would be back in a few months when the fighting was over.

He hadn't mentioned which side he was joining. Kentucky, although a slave state, had not seceded from the Union and had declared itself neutral. As a result, Kentucky men and boys were joining both the Union and the Confederacy. The plain truth was Jamison Jakes didn't know which side he would join, nor did he really care. He knew nothing of the issues dividing the nation. He'd never been more than a few miles from home and then only to hunt or fish or go with his father to haul tobacco to auction. Once, while with his father in Lexington, he had seen Negroes being bought and sold on the slave blocks, and this had bothered him some. His father had told him to never mind; it was none of their concern.

Jakes' first thought after leaving home was to head for Lexington to enlist. He started in that direction but then suspected Lexington would be the first place his father would go looking, so he traveled north. It took him almost two days of getting lost and getting back on track to reach the village of Georgetown. It was almost nightfall when he finally saw the village's flickering lights, so he decided to bed down and wait until morning before going in.

He built a small fire and was warming himself, nibbling on his last biscuit, when a figure stepped into the light.

"Mind if I share your fire?" asked a cheery voice.

"Who might you be?" responded a startled Jakes.

"Name's Dickie Hubbard. I'm sure 'nuf bushed. Got some jerky I'll trade you for a side of your fire."

The thought of any kind of meat, even jerky, was enough to make Jakes hospitable. And, if the truth be known, he was very lonely and more than a little homesick.

"What you doin' out here by yourself?" Hubbard asked.

"On my way to join up."

"Hey, me too. Hear they's recruitin' in Georgetown. I'm goin' in at first light. It'll be good us goin' in together. Maybe if I learn to like you, I'll save your life someday in a big battle."

"Which side you gonna join?" asked Jamison Jakes in hopes of getting a handle on his own decision.

"Don't rightly know" came the unhelpful reply. "Got one brother wearin' the blue and another wearin' the gray. Don't know it matters all that much so long's I get in before the fun's over with."

The talk went into the night. Two young, soon-to-be warriors set for battle, eager to be in the thick of it, to wear a uniform and march in formation, to save each other's lives if need be, to bleed and maybe die before they had really lived. These were important matters for two sixteen-year-olds to discuss as they shared a fire and beef jerky on a chilly night they thought would never end.

With the first glow of dawn, the new friends were strolling down Georgetown's main street.

"I wonder if they feed you as soon as you join up?" Hubbard asked with a grin.

"Don't know," Jakes replied, "but, Lord, I hope so."

Although Kentucky was officially neutral regarding the

war, many Kentuckians died on their home soil, at the hands of both sides. Two of Kentucky's native sons -- Abraham Lincoln and Jefferson Davis -- led the opposing factions. Ironically, while fighting was supposedly not allowed in the state, the recruiting of soldiers for both sides was permitted, and the competition for inductees was fierce.

On that early morning in Georgetown, the recruiting officers had to shout to be heard over the blaring of attention-getting brass bands. On one corner "Yankee Doodle Dandy" was playing, while a block away, "Dixie" was going strong. Jamison Jakes and Dickie Hubbard stood first in front of the Union recruiting table and listened as a burly sergeant promised them each a free horse and rifle at the end of the war, and a new pair of shoes immediately. The Confederates made no promises, offering nothing in return for signing up. This answered the question, at least in part, why the Union enlistment line was three times longer than the Confederates'.

Dickie Hubbard asked the question which decided the matter. "If we join up, will you give us breakfast?" Politics aside, Jamison Jakes and Dickie Hubbard became Confederate privates, no questions asked, in exchange for two hard-boiled eggs, a thin slice of bacon, three biscuits and a hot cup of coffee.

Later in the day Jakes and Hubbard were split up, being assigned to units headed in different directions. That was the last they were to see each other, but many times in the years that followed Jakes thought of his comrade, their brief time together, and the wisdom of their decision. At those times he would smile and slowly shake his head.

Jakes proved to be a good soldier. He was wounded once, but out of action for only a week. He became hardened, learning to accept death as a matter of course. As time went on, he understood the political and economic differences between the North and South. But he never really figured out why he, Jamison Jakes, was fighting.

At the end of the war he served as an honor guard to

General Lee when he surrendered to Grant at Appomattox Court House. Two weeks later, when General Johnston surrendered his army to Sherman, Jakes was mustered out of the Army of the Confederacy, given a horse without a saddle, and told to go home in peace.

It took him almost two weeks to cross the mountains and reach central Kentucky's rolling hills. Arriving at what was once a tenant farmer's small tobacco field, there was no one to welcome him. Behind a pile of blackened rubble that had been the family home, Jamison Jakes found seven mounds of dirt and a rough handmade sign that read simply, "Jakes Family." A band of marauding Bushwhackers had run roughshod through the Bluegrass region, killing everyone and burning everything in their path. In that moment of great sadness, Jamison Jakes realized the bigness of the world and the smallness of a man left in it alone. He camped for a few days near their graves, visiting there with his family to relate stories of battles won and lost; to apologize time and again for running away from home; and to speak tearfully of the wasted, bloody years that had been his rite of passage from boyhood to manhood.

He pulled weeds from each mound of red earth and transplanted wildflowers in a large circle around his family's final resting place. Before riding off, he sat for a long while at the foot of what he guessed to be his mother's grave and asked her forgiveness for not writing. Looking briefly at the space beyond the last dirt mound, the one that would have been his had he not left home, a thorn of guilt stabbed his gut. He was glad to be alive.

Jakes stayed around Lexington for a few days, was offered a job in a general store and seriously considered working as a linesman for the telegraph company. He passed on both offers, pointed his horse west and looked straight ahead.

Chapter 3

The pounding on the hotel room door brought Jamison Jakes back from reflecting on events of more than a dozen years before.

"You gonna sleep the night in that tub?" the agitated maid asked. "We got someone else waitin' for it."

He spent the next few hours in restless sleep. Too many dreams about too many mistakes in his life. At age thirty-four he had nothing tangible to show for years of hard work as a vagabond handyman. Maybe he would have fared better as a Lexington telegraph linesman. Chances are he would have a family by now.

Jakes was a pragmatist, playing the hand dealt without much complaint. He shunned trouble when he could and was satisfied with making a dollar any legal way possible. His decision to keep heading west was made in much the same way he made all his decisions. A wagon master leading a train from Frankfort to the plains of Kansas needed someone to scout, so Jakes signed on for three squares a day and the promise of twenty dollars at the end of the trail.

Scouting for a wagon train offered little adventure. He would ride out a few hours ahead of the group, find an overnight camp site, and gather firewood for cooking that day's supper and the next morning's breakfast. Changing jobs was an easy decision for Jakes after the Conestogas had delivered the farmers to central Kansas.

Other than the time he served in the army, being a cowhand was much harder work than any he ever tried, but it was steady and the men he rode with were likeable enough. Still, the most exciting part of starting his first roundup and drive was the thought of its being over. Then he would have money to spend, a hot bath, and clean clothes.

Jakes shook off the thoughts of his restless night by planning his first full day in Cheyenne. He would put on clean clothes, get a big order of steak and eggs, and find a barber.

The doors to the Hobson House café were just opening as Jakes reached the hotel lobby. Two guests were waiting impatiently and mumbling about how city folk must not get hungry until after six in the morning and that half a day had been wasted waiting for breakfast to be served. Jakes smiled his agreement but declined their offer to join them, choosing rather to sit alone at a table in the corner of the small room.

In the middle of his third cup of coffee, a man entered the café, pulled up a chair at a neighboring table, and sat down. He was an old man with a craggy face and a long, drooping gray moustache that matched perfectly his shoulder-length hair. His blue eyes met Jakes' and held them for a moment. As the man was taking his seat, Jakes noticed he was wearing two pistols slung low in holsters tied down with rawhide.

The old man didn't look like a cowhand. His palms weren't calloused, his gleaming white shirt was accented by a small black string tie, and his boots, while not new, were clear of scuffs and cuts. Before starting to look at a few sheets of paper he had unrolled, the man placed a pair of gold-rimmed reading glasses carefully on his nose.

The man couldn't help noticing he was being studied by Jamison Jakes, and before Jakes could look away, the old man gave him a slight smile that said, "Your turn will come, young man. Age has a way of standing still and letting you catch up." Finishing his coffee and passing the old man's table on the way to the door, Jakes nodded and returned the smile, but said nothing.

The bright orange rays of the morning sun were pouring light into the musty hotel lobby as Jakes entered from the café. Inside the lobby, he was startled to see the desk clerk, face milky white, both hands high in the air, shaking visibly. A tall man in a long duster was waving a rifle in front of the clerk.

"What the hell's goin' on?" Jakes shouted, reaching for his Colt.

Before his seldom-drawn pistol had time to clear its holster, Jakes felt a sharp pain across the side of his skull. Half spinning, he hit the floor and took the full force of a kick to his ribs. As his mind raced toward blackness, he was aware of a blurry figure standing over him and heard the sound of a hammer being cocked. He instinctively rolled onto his side, pulled his knees up to his chest, placed both arms tightly around his head, and waited to die. Two shots in quick succession rang out. The last recollection Jakes had was of a weight falling across his body.

From a place he thought must be eternity, Jakes could hear the muffled sounds of words coming from cotton-filled mouths. He could make out some of them. "Lucky." "Split scalp." "Gonna be okay." After some minutes of trying to keep his head from spinning off his neck, he was able to pry open his eyes.

"Where am I?"

"In your hotel room. You took a real beatin' and near got

yourself shot. If that ol' man hadn't come to your rescue, we'd be plantin' you now instead of talkin' to you."

"Somebody light the lamp," Jakes said. "It's too dark in here to make out who you are."

"My Lord! That bump on your head must be causin' you real trouble. It's only a bit after noon and the sun's brighter than it's been in days."

Immediate panic seized Jamison Jakes.

"Blind!" He yelled. "I'm blind!"

"Hey, hey. Take it easy, fella. Could be a lot worse. You could be dead, remember."

"Are you a doctor?" asked Jakes, beginning to calm a bit.

"Nope, I'm the hotel desk clerk. The doc will be here soon. He's out to the McSorley place. He'll be back in a couple of hours and we'll make sure he gets right on over here."

"Where's the man who saved my life?"

"Don't rightly know. We was too busy gettin' you took care of to notice. I seen him talkin' to the sheriff -- 'bout the shootin', I reckon. Man, that was really somethin'. That old man walked smack in the middle of that stickup with both guns drawn and plugged both them hombres at the same time, and they was on different sides of the lobby."

"Would you see if you can find him? I'd really want to thank him for savin' my skin."

"I'll see if I can round him up. Now you best try to get some rest 'til Doc gets up here. I'll make sure someone looks in on you from time to time."

With the click of the door latch, Jamison Jakes was again filled with anxiety. He had known men blinded in the war. He had watched them groping and stumbling and begging God to let them see again. Was this to be his fate?

In the heat of the early afternoon, Jakes lay in his bed and allowed his mind to wander back through the years to happier times...and sadder. He thought of a woman's last words to him.

Were those words simply coincidental, or were they a portent?
"Jamison Jakes, you're a fool! A blind fool!"

He had met Hannah Robbins on the wagon train from Kentucky to Kansas. Her mother was a large rawboned woman and her father a fragile pale man who seemed ill-fitted to begin a life as a Kansas sodbuster. Hannah inherited physical traits from both of them. She was tall like her mother, but not large, with the pale, delicate features of her father. In all, she was a handsome young woman.

The relationship started off innocently enough. A lost hub nut from the wheel of the Robbins' wagon resulted in a repair job for Jakes. By the time the nut was found and the wheel replaced it was almost dark, so Jakes and the Robbins family camped some miles behind the rest of the train. Hannah cooked the supper. It may have been the lateness of the hour or the appetite that had been worked up during the long day, but that supper was the best Jamison Jakes could remember having in a long time.

His compliment to Hannah brought a quick response from her mother. "And she can sew just as good!"

During the days that followed, Jakes readily accepted the many invitations to have supper at the Robbins' wagon. The weekly hoedowns that broke the boredom of the pilgrims' travels also became important to Jakes. And to Hannah. And to Hannah's mother. By the time the wagon train reached Missouri, it seemed to many that Hannah Robbins and Jamison Jakes were seriously courting.

They never talked of marriage, but there was an expectation, especially on the part of Mrs. Robbins, that when the train reached Kansas and a preacher could be found, Hannah would become Mrs. Jamison Jakes. Even Mr. Robbins was comfortable in calling Jakes "son."

Jakes' comfort level, however, decreased considerably the closer the wagons got to Kansas, and during the last week of the journey he spent more and more time doing scouting chores and less and less time hanging around the Robbins' wagon. The night before the train reached its ending point, Jakes and Hannah took a long walk on the moonlit prairie. The girl spoke first.

"Jamison, do you love me?"

"Guess maybe I do."

"Then what's the matter? What's wrong?"

"There's nothin' wrong. Just got a lot on my mind."

"Would you share it with me?"

"Nothin' to share. I don't mean no disrespect, Hannah, but there's some things I just got to keep to myself."

"I don't understand. If two people are in love and planning to spend the rest of their lives together, there can be no secrets."

"They're not secrets, really. I just can't share some of the things I think."

"Jamison, please try. It's important that I know everything about you. It isn't fair for you not to tell me what you're thinking."

"Even if it'll hurt you?"

"Hurt me? What could you possibly say that would hurt me?"

"That I don't wanna get married. The thought of gettin' married and settlin' down and havin' kids scares the livin' daylights outta me. I never asked you to marry me, and I don't think I've done or said anything that made you think I wanted to. I listened to your ma make plans and I kept quiet instead of speakin' up like I should've. I just figured so long as we were on the trail I wouldn't have to face up to my scaredness and somehow it would go away."

"I can't believe what I'm hearing," Hannah Robbins said angrily. "I can't believe you would spend all that time with me acting like you loved me if you didn't mean anything by it. What will I do now? There are other men on this train that I could've spent my time with. Honorable men who know how to treat a woman. Now my chance to marry one of them is gone! I'm out here on this god-forsaken plain with an overbearing mother and a mouse of a father and I'll never have a chance to spend time with any man I'd ever be interested in marrying. Why are you doing this to me? Those nights I watched you sleep by our campfire would make me dream of the nights we would spend together. Now you tell me you don't want to get married! What am I going to do?"

Jamison Jakes wanted to reach out and take the sobbing girl in his arms and tell her he was mistaken, that those were not his thoughts at all, that he did want to marry her and settle down and have children. But which was the real scare and which was false? Did he really love her? Enough to marry? What was it he was beginning to feel as she expressed her disappointment? Love...? Pity...? Guilt...?

So he did or said nothing more. He simply followed the tall, slender woman to her wagon and quietly saddled his horse. Riding into the night, he heard the woman who had planned to be his wife and the mother of his children shouting after him.

"You're a fool, Jamison Jakes! A blind fool!"

Chapter 4

He couldn't determine the time of day when the doctor finally arrived, so he asked.

"It's around four o'clock," a thin voice responded. "You the doc?"

"Well, some people think I am when they need help having a baby, or they've got themselves shot for some reason, or no reason, or if they got their head busted like you."

"I don't give a damn about my head, Doc. It's my eyes. Am I gonna stay blind?"

"I can't rightly tell how bad it is at this point. Judging from that lump, and the dent in your skull, your brains are sure shaken up. Since you can't see anything already, your vision won't get any worse. Might even clear up if you allow enough time."

"I can't just lay here, Doc. I'll go crazy just layin' here in the dark with nothin' to do."

"You can maybe be up and around for a bit tomorrow, long enough to go down to the café for a good meal. Main thing to remember is to keep your head as still as you can. You're going to need someone to help you get around so you don't hurt yourself even more. Is there someone around here who can help you? Did you ride in with anyone?"

"All the fellas I rode in with have headed home. Doc, I don't know one person in all of Cheyenne. I don't even know the name of a person."

Jakes felt totally disheartened. It was bad enough to be alone, even when things were smooth. The thought of being alone *and* blind was a double load.

"Doc, I'm scared."

"Of course you are. That's to be expected. I'll nose around and see if I can find someone to be your eyes. But for now, you've got to rest. I won't tell you not to be scared or not to worry, because I honestly don't know what's going to happen. There's a real good man I know in Denver who's a specialist in dealing with these problems. I'll get on the telegraph to him and see what he thinks. Your head must be in a world of hurt, so I'm leaving a bottle of pain tonic here on the nightstand. Take a good swig every couple of hours. I'll look in on you when I can."

The doctor's words were less than reassuring, but they did remove some of Jakes' panic. If there was a doctor in Denver who knew how to treat these things, then other people must have the same problem. But what if the doc couldn't find someone willing to be a guide? Even if he could, what kind of man needs to be lead around by the hand and told where not to step, be spoon fed at meals, and be pointed in the right direction when it was time to piss?

"A blind man, that's who," Jakes said aloud, answering his own silent questions.

After some fumbling, he found the tonic bottle, opened it and took a big swallow of the bitter liquid. Then he lay back and stared toward the ceiling and tried to remember if it had a pattern or if it was plain.

"Are you awake?" The doctor entered the room without knocking.

"That you, Doc? Yeah, I'm awake."

"Found you some help. He'll be up in a shake. Young fellow looking to earn the price of a meal or two. Said he'd be hanging around town until the end of the week. He's a real wiseacre, but he's the best I can find right now."

"I think I met him already," replied Jakes, remembering the sassy kid in the saloon. "I'm not sure he'll work out, Doc."

"Well, I'll keep looking in case he gets to be a handful."

"Did you hear from the Denver man yet?"

"I sent the message, but haven't had time to get an answer. Hope to have something by morning. Let me take a look."

The doctor lit the lamp and moved it close to Jakes' head.

"The lump's gone down some," the doctor said. "That's a good sign."

"Hey, Doc! I can tell when you move the lamp! It's really dim, but I can see the light move!"

"Well, sir, I'd say that's another good sign," responded the doctor. "You must be starving. If that boy doesn't get here soon, I'll go down to the café and tote something back for you to sink your teeth into."

"Never you mind, sawbones, I'm here," said a voice from the doorway.

Jamison Jakes could hear the sound of what he guessed were large Mexican spurs, made purposely to jingle, as the young man made his way across the room.

"Well, I swear iffen it ain't the man who done the preachin' at me last night!"

"Hello, youngster," said Jakes, trying to sound as cheerful as possible. "Didn't think I'd ever see you again."

"I reckon by all rights, you *ain't* seen me again. That is, if I can believe ol' Doc here who says you're blind as a coot."

"Now hold on there," protested the doctor. "I never said a thing like that, and you know it. Why don't you put a rein on that fast mouth?"

"Hey, Doc, it's okay," Jakes cautioned. "If his eyes are as sharp as his tongue, he should be able to get me around real well."

"All right, Mister Jakes, if you say so. But I'm going to keep looking for someone else."

With that, the doctor closed his bag, placed a second bottle of tonic on the nightstand, and left with the promise that he would return early the next morning. As the door closed behind the doctor, Jakes looked toward where he thought the young man was standing.

"I don't think we got properly introduced last night in the saloon. Name's Jamison Jakes."

"An' I'm the Alamo Kid. My granddaddy was Davy Crockett, so I figger I got a right to go by that handle."

Even the youth's tone of voice had a swagger to it.

"Well, Alamo Kid, do you think you can find the slop jar? I'm dyin' to take a leak."

Jamison Jakes slept surprisingly well during the night. Maybe it was the hot supper that had been brought to the room. Maybe it was because he knew the Alamo Kid was sleeping on the floor next to the bed. Jakes had always been a loner. But then, he had never needed anyone before.

"Hey, Kid," Jakes said softly. "You awake?"

"Sure am, Preacher. Glad to hear you makin' noises. Thought maybe you'd done gone to the happy huntin' grounds."

"If the café's open, I wanna go downstairs and get some breakfast," Jakes said. "Can't stand to be cooped up here any longer."

Walking through the hallway, down a flight of stairs, across the lobby and into the café, Jakes could imagine the stares that must have followed the two. A man with a large bandage on his head being led by a kid with clanging spurs.

Once seated, Jakes shifted attention to his hunger.

"What're you gonna have for breakfast, Kid?" asked Jakes.

"I ain't much on breakfast, Preacher. I'll just have whatever you're gittin'."

"The menu's written there on the wall, Kid. Does it say if they're servin' biscuits and redeye gravy?"

"Yessir, plenty a' that," responded the Kid immediately.

Jakes could hear the heavy footsteps of the cook as he came to the table to get their order.

"Mornin', Mister Jakes," said a gravely voice. "Sure was somethin' the way you went after them banditos yesterday. Folks are sayin' if you hadn't slowed them two down, they would've got away with everythin' in the hotel safe. I been told your money ain't no good in here. All your meals are on the house so long as you're laid up. That goes for your sidekick here, too."

"Well, that's really great!" said Jakes with a broad smile. "That bein' the case, bring us both a double order of biscuits and redeye gravy."

"I'm real sorry, but all we got is what's written on that wall over there and it don't say we're servin' biscuits and gravy. Now, biscuits I got, but I never learnt the knack of makin' gravy. Always come out too lumpy or too thin or too somethin'. How's 'bout a big T-bone steak and some eggs?"

"That'll be fine. Two platters of those and a big basket of the biscuits."

As the cook returned to the kitchen, Jamison Jakes and the Alamo Kid sat in silence. Jakes broke the quiet.

"You can't read can you, Kid?"

"Sure I can read. I can read real good. There's a word on that wall that I mistook fer gravy. I can read real good. And I can write, too. My ma made sure I could read an' write, an' I can do my numbers. I can do my numbers real good. Even iffen I couldn't, I'd be better off than you. What's the use of knowin' how to read or write or do numbers iffen you're blind? Tell me that, Preacher man."

"No use at all, Kid. No use at all."

As they were finishing breakfast, the doctor came in, pulled up a chair, and sat between Jakes and the Kid.

"Got an answer from my man in Denver," the doctor began. "He can't tell a thing about your condition without being able to give you a complete going over. Wants you to get on down to Denver just as soon as you're able to travel. That should be in a couple of days."

Jamison Jakes looked in the direction of the Alamo Kid.

"What about it, Kid? Think you could get us to Denver?"

"Only if you promise to preach no more'n one sermon a day," came a quick response from the Alamo Kid.

Chapter 5

It took three days before the doctor finally gave Jakes the okay to make the trip to Denver. The morning he was leaving, a number of townsfolk crowded into the café to say goodbye and wish him well. They'd passed the hat the day before, collecting more than two hundred dollars to help pay the costs of the Denver specialist. Such were the feelings of the Cheyenne people for their heroes.

Jamison Jakes and the Alamo Kid presented an almost comical picture as they rode out of town. The Kid took the lead with the reins of Jakes' horse tied to the tail of the Kid's pinto. "All you need do, Preacher, is stay in the saddle. I'll do the drivin'."

They decided to follow the stage route to Denver. It would take longer, but since the Alamo Kid had never been that direction and Jakes was in no condition to help, they figured they would be less likely to get lost by staying on the road.

Their journey would take them to the outpost of Fort Collins, from there to the mining town of Boulder, and finally into Denver, a distance of about a hundred and thirty miles. Not wanting to push the horses more than thirty miles a day, they planned to spend the better part of a week the road, including a little extra drinking time in Fort Collins and Boulder.

The trip was filled with beauty. Each sunrise, the high plains country radiated like an Old World master spreading his canvas on the horizon and liberally splashing hues of deep red, orange, and pink across the sky, then adding a wash of purple in the evening. Herds of antelope grazed their way down the mountains, getting ready for winter. Beavers splashed happily as they built dams in the slow-running brooks. Pine trees, mixed with fir and alder, provided perfect complements to the thin aspens with their yellow leaves fraily clinging to their branches. At night, a full moon banished the darkness so completely that firewood could be gathered with little difficulty. Even the howls of the coyotes provided solace rather than concern.

The Alamo Kid, sensitive to Jamison Jakes' feelings, tried to keep all he was seeing to himself, but occasionally he would forget and let out a "Wow, would you look at that!" Even so, Jakes was aware, through his ears and nose and the feel of the fresh air blowing across his face, that he was missing many visual splendors.

It was due in large part to this awareness that, as the days wore on, Jakes let his mind dwell on the possibility he would never see again. From the first night of his blindness, and each night thereafter, he would fall asleep believing the next morning he would wake up and be able to see. Each morning brought another disappointment and the rest of the day Jakes' feared that he would always be blind. These thoughts drove him to feelings bordering on serious depression, much to the discomfort of the Alamo Kid.

"Hell, Preacher," he complained, "you're 'bout as much fun to be 'round as a calf with the colic."

On the day they were to reach Denver, Jamison Jakes' depression ran out of control. He had bought three bottles of whiskey during their stop in Boulder and held one clinched tightly in his fist from the time the two broke camp in the dewy morning until they stopped for lunch.

"What you been doin' with that bottle?" asked a surprised Alamo Kid, realizing Jakes was unable to dismount at the rest stop.

"What you think I been doin' with this bottle, you dumb little shit?" slurred Jamison Jakes. "I been makin' love to it."

"That ain't the smartest thing to be doin'," retorted the Kid. "What the hell's botherin' you, Preacher?"

"I'm not a preacher and if you call me that one more time you better be ready to fight! What's botherin' me? You stupid piss-ant runt! I'm blind! And I'm tired of bein' blind. I'm tired of havin' to be led around by some snot-nosed brat. I know I'm never gonna see again. I'm gonna spend the rest of my life sittin' in some home where they'll feed me twice a day and read me the newspaper and wipe my ass and comb my hair. That's not livin'; that's breathin' death. I ain't gonna spend the rest of my miserable life that way. I'm just not! Thanks for everthin' you've done for me, Kid. Take what money's left; you earned it."

At the end of his drunken monologue, Jamison Jakes pulled the Colt from its holster and tried to cock the hammer, at the same time attempting to put the gun barrel in his mouth. Before he could do either, the Kid pulled Jakes from his horse, grabbed the pistol and slapped Jakes hard with the back of his hand.

"You bastard!" screamed the Kid. "You chicken-livered bastard! Poor you. Can't see, so's you wanna take the sissy way out. I don't know one thing 'bout you, mister, 'cept I know I like you. I don't know why, but I do. I thought we was in this together. I was your eyes an' you needed me. What am I gonna do iffen you blow your brains out? One thing I won't do! I sure as hell won't bury you. I'll leave you here to be picked apart by the coyotes and buzzards."

With that, the Alamo Kid placed the pistol back in Jakes' hand.

"At least do me a favor. Wait 'til I ride off 'fore you do it." The rustling of the horse told Jamison Jakes that the Kid was in the saddle.

"Kid, wait! Don't leave me!"

"Why not? You're ready to leave me."

"I know. I'm sorry. Please get me to Denver."

Jakes was aware the Alamo Kid had dismounted and was standing next to him.

"It's the whiskey, Kid. I sometimes don't handle it too good."

"Yeah, I know. Sometimes I got a problem handlin' my corn, too."

Jamison Jakes felt the hand of the Alamo Kid squeeze his arm.

"Hey, Preacher, you're gonna see again. I'd bet my last sawbuck on it."

It was dusk when the two weary travelers finally reached Denver. They were both saddle-sore, and Jakes had worn blisters on his hands from holding so tightly to his saddle horn. They'd had to stop twice for Jakes to throw up from the whiskey. All things considered, Jamison Jakes was eager to find a bed.

Not knowing what the specialist would charge for his services, Jakes asked the Kid to find a hotel that was "clean but cheap." The Kid chose the Nugget Inn, not so much for its cleanliness or its cheapness. It seemed to have the busiest saloon in town.

The two settled in their room and the Alamo Kid went to the hotel's café and returned with a bowl of barley soup for Jakes. The long silence that followed was broken by Jamison Jakes.

"That was a stupid-assed thing I did out there today, Kid."

"No doubt 'bout that, Preacher."

"You know what it's like to be scared, Kid? I mean, really scared? I was in the army durin' the war and was in a lotta scrapes. Some real big ones. But that was different. There were hundreds of men around and all were just as scared as the next; but nobody let on so the scare passed real quick. Then there'd be times when we were too busy fightin' to be scared. But this thing -- this blindness -- is different. I'm just here, all wrapped up inside myself. I only got me to live with hour after hour. When you're not around makin' noises, I wonder if there's anythin' there, like the world has just gone off and left me. That's a different kind of scared, one I can't do nothin' about. Know what I mean, Kid?"

The Alamo Kid's large spurs jangled as he slowly paced the floor, then he stopped and slumped heavily into an overstuffed chair.

"Yeah, Preacher, I know a little a' what you mean 'bout bein' scared an' not bein' able to do nothin' 'bout it. You got your blindness. I had my old man. God, he was a mean somebitch. There weren't no pleasin' him. An' when he weren't pleased, he took it out on the nearest person. He was forever beatin' up on Ma, an' when I'd try to jump in an' help her, it'd be a double dose fer me."

The Kid was starting to breathe hard as he went on. "I 'member once Pa told me to grub a whole field a' spuds one day when he went to town. Well, sir, I was downright 'termined I was gonna git that job done to his likin' iffen it killed me. So I grubbed an' hauled an' worked without stoppin' to eat or nothin'. When he got back, it was well past dark, an' I hadda take the coal oil lamp out to the 'tater patch so's he could see I got 'em all dug an' hauled away 'cept for two hills. That old fart didn't say a word to me. Just turned on his heels an' went to the house fer the strap. All the time he was beatin' me, he was yellin' how I was a no-good lazy bum."

The Alamo Kid was glad that Jamison Jakes couldn't see the tears in his eyes.

"I was just seven years old, an' that was a real big 'tater patch. So I done had my own kinda fear, not knowin' when I might say somethin' to set him off. I'd go hide in the corner when he come into the room. I was always a' feared fer Ma, an' I'd watch her face get all pale when he took out after her.

"If he'd been a Bible-thumper, I s'pose he coulda claimed the Lord made him do it. They was a lotta that goin' 'round. But we never had no Bible in the house. Wouldn't a done no good iffen we did, 'cause he couldn't read.

"Anyways, I think I killed him. I prayed every night he'd croak but he was just too mean to die. Couple months ago, he was at Ma again with a butcher knife an' he was holdin' her down an' fixin' to cut her. I picked up a ax handle an' hit him 'cross the back a' the head an' he fell like a shot hog.

"Then Ma commenced screamin' how I'd killed him an' she picked up the knife an' started after me. So I run to the barn as quick as I could an' saddled my pony an' got the hell outta there. I don't know iffen he's dead. I hope to God he is. I jump ever time I hear a noise, thinkin' he's right behind me.

"Yeah, I know what scared is. But I ain't never gonna back down from no one ever again. I'm as tough as the next guy, an' anyone who stands in my way's gonna find that out. Someday I'm gonna be somebody. People are gonna respect me an' they're gonna step aside when I pass 'em on the sidewalk, an' my drinks are gonna be free in any saloon 'cause everyone'll wanna be a friend of the Alamo Kid."

With this, the Kid and Jakes became lost in their own thoughts and the world was quiet again. Morning found the Kid sleeping in the chair where he'd sat the night before and Jakes looking blankly toward a ceiling he couldn't see.

Chapter 6

It was the Alamo Kid's job to locate the Denver specialist. Jamison Jakes had the name and address scrawled on a piece of paper given to him by the doctor in Cheyenne, and the Kid left before breakfast to try to find the miracle man who would give Jakes back his sight.

"Don't be too stubborn to ask for directions," Jakes told the Kid as he was leaving. "This is a big town and findin' one man may be hard to come by without a little help."

Shortly after the Kid left, there was a knock on the door.

"Who is it?" Jakes asked in a loud voice.

"My name's Maryalice. I work here in the hotel. I have breakfast for you."

"I didn't order any breakfast," Jakes said, with some annoyance. "You must have the wrong room."

"No, I don't, Mister Jakes. The young man you're traveling with asked me to bring you something to eat."

"Okay, wait just a minute." Jakes fumbled around to make sure his pants were buttoned, ran his fingers through his hair a few times, pulled on his shirt, and announced, "You can come in now."

As the door opened, Jakes' nostrils filled with a fragrance of sweet perfume mixed delightfully with the aroma of steak and eggs, fried potatoes, biscuits and hot coffee.

"I'll just put this tray down here on the table, Mister Jakes, and you can dig in."

"Excuse me, ma'am. There's a little problem here. I can't see. Didn't the Kid tell you I was blind? I need help when I eat. I don't know why he had you bring all this stuff."

"Oh, he didn't. He said to bring you something in a bowl that you could eat with a spoon. It was my idea to bring you what's here. Yes, I know you're blind but I suspect there's nothing wrong with your hands. And your elbows seem to bend just fine. There's no reason for even a blind man to go through life eating soup and mush."

"Well, that food sure smells good and after all those days of eatin' what the Kid threw together on the trail, I surely do wanna sink my teeth into a good hunk of meat. Could you feed me? I mean, if you don't have other chores to do right away."

"I really can't stay, Mister Jakes. But you won't have any trouble eating. I'll cut the steak into pieces for you, but everything else you can do for yourself. Think of your plate as a big clock. Your steak is at twelve, your eggs are at three, and the potatoes are at six. Your coffee is just off the side at two, and the biscuits at ten. The coffee pot is straight ahead of you about six inches from the top of the plate. When you want to pour more, put your thumb with the first knuckle on the rim of the cup and the end of your thumb down inside. When the coffee reaches your thumb, stop pouring.

"I'll be back after a while to pick up your tray. I've got water heating in the tub room, so when you've finished eating I'll take you there and you can get scrubbed up. After that, if your friend isn't back, I'll take you across the street to the barber shop. I know you really could use a shave."

Before Jakes could utter a protest, a thank you, or a

goodbye, the door closed with a quiet click and the woman was gone. Only her perfume remained.

Jamison Jakes was amazed at how easy it was to eat following Maryalice's instructions to think of his plate as a clock. If worse came to worse and he stayed blind, maybe with a lot of practice, he might learn to lead a somewhat normal life.

As promised, Maryalice returned later to tell Jakes his bath was ready, that she would bring along his change of clothes, and led him to the tub room. Once inside, Maryalice gave specific instructions. "Feel this chair? I put your clean clothes here. This is the tub. Just drop your dirty clothes where you stand. The water in the tub is about two feet deep. Step over the side of the tub with your left leg. The fuzzy stuff you'll feel in the water is bubbles; I put some of my bubble-bath soap in the water to make the scrubbing easier. Don't worry, it doesn't have any smell to it, it just feels good. I'll lock the door when I leave so no one will disturb you. I'll be back to unlock it when I think you've soaked enough. Oh, yes, and there's a little tray at the foot of the tub with a large bar of lye soap and a washcloth. Make sure they both get used. Do you have any questions?"

Before he could answer, once again Jakes heard the click of a closing door and the rattle as it locked from the outside.

As with eating breakfast, by following Maryalice's instructions, he had no trouble getting into the tub and finding the soap and washcloth and he knew he would be able to find his clothes when he was ready to get dressed. He allowed himself to relax for the first time in the many terrible days since he lost his sight. He craved a cheroot and a glass of Platte River whiskey

Jakes was startled from his half-sleep in the tub by the noise of the door being unlocked.

"Whoa, wait a minute! I'm still in the tub!"

"Oh, I'm glad for that," replied Maryalice in a soft voice. "I forgot to leave you any towels. I bet you would have gotten lost in the dark looking for towels that weren't here. Anyway, you probably need some help getting your back scrubbed."

Before Jamison Jakes could speak, the woman was kneeling beside the tub.

"Now hand me the washcloth and soap."

Jakes was not about to move his hands from where he had placed them, providing coverage of his manliness.

"I can't see where they are, ma'am, you'll have to find them."

"Mister Jakes, you can see where they are as readily as I can. And don't worry about my seeing any of your well-kept secrets. I've been blind myself since I was four years old."

The Alamo Kid, returning to the hotel shortly after noon, found Jamison Jakes sipping coffee at a table in the corner of the café. "Woooee! Ain't you a purty sight!" shouted the Kid when he saw Jakes' clean-shaven face, fresh clothes and polished boots. "You fixin' to go to church?"

"Hi, Kid," Jakes responded with a backward flick of his hand. "Pull up a chair and have some coffee."

"Coffee, hell! I need me 'bout four fingers a' strong corn. I never come so close to gittin' killed so many times in one day ever. Can't believe all the people in this here town. An' horses an' buggies an' great big covered wagons that people git on an' off up an' down the streets. I swear, I was a' feared to try an' cross a street.

"And folks ain't none too friendly neither. I kept tryin' to git someone to tell me how to find the doc's office, but they just plain paid me no nevermind. After a bit I got downright mad at gittin' no help, so's I went in a store an' handed the man who was clerkin' that piece a' paper with the doc's address on it an' told him I'd be most obliged iffen he'd tell me how to find the place I was lookin' fer. Since he was starin' down my gun barrel at the time, he got real friendly, real fast."

"So, you found him? You found the doc?" Jamison Jakes could do little to hide his excitement.

"Yep, sure did. He thought he was too busy to see you today, but after him and me had a little talk he said to bring you in at day's end an' he'd have a look-see."

"Did you pull your gun on him, too? Damn it, Kid, you can't go through life havin' your own way just 'cause you got a fist full of iron."

"Yeah, you may think you can't. But the job gits did don't it? I didn't ride the skin offa my ass to come down here an' listen to someone tell me to come back when he's ready fer me to come back. Tomorrow or the next day may be fine fer him, but not fer me. An' I'd think that wouldn't be fine with you neither."

"Hold on a minute, Kid," Jakes said in a calmer voice. "I really appreciate it that he'll see me today. I just don't want to get off on the wrong foot, that's all. I want him to like me so he'll do everything he can to make me see. I don't want him to write me off 'cause we got started all a-kilter."

"Hell, Jamison, he ain't allowed to do that. He took some kinda oath or somethin' where he promised to look after people whether he liked 'em or not. Now, you add to that the fact that you're the number-one special friend a' the Alamo Kid an' you got a combine that'll git you real good service." The Kid had a smile in his voice and seemed to savor drawing out the word "good."

"Okay, Kid, you win. Just know when to slap leather and when not to." Then Jakes added, changing the subject, "What time of day is it gettin' to be? What time did the doc say to be at his office?"

"I'd fix the time 'round two," guessed the Alamo Kid. "The doc'll be lookin' fer us sometime 'bout six."

"That should give you plenty of time to get yourself a bath then, Kid."

"A bath? It ain't Saturday night, is it? I only take a bath on a Saturday night."

"Then you got a choice to make. You can either pretend it's one of the Saturday nights you've missed since I've known you, or you can sleep in the barn with the horses. It's okay bein' in the same room when we both stink, but I'm not about to be the only one in there that doesn't smell."

"Well, I don't cotton none to sleepin' in the stable. You want me to take you back upstairs 'fore I order the tub?"

"No thanks, Kid. I'll be fine right here. And say, Kid, do you see that woman around anywhere, the one you had bring my breakfast?"

"Sure do, Preacher," responded the Alamo Kid after a few seconds of scanning the room. "She's standin' over there by the kitchen door talkin' to some fat man."

"Tell me what she looks like."

"Well, sir, I figger her to be a foot shorter'n you. Her hair's 'bout the same color as your horse's mane. Hangs down to her waist. Her skin's dark from bein' out in the sun a lot. Looks like from here she's gotta mole on her cheek. It ain't no ugly mole. It's like one that them dancehall girls paint on. 'Cept this one's real."

"And her clothes, Kid. Tell me what she's wearin'."

"She's got on a skirt made outta calico, or gingham. I never knowed the difference 'tween them two. It's mostly red with some black thread runnin' through it. She's wearin' a white blouse with red buttons an' she's got leather sandals. Oh, yeah, she's got a red bow in her hair. Just a small one, bein' held in with a little comb. That 'bout does it. Iffen you like, I can sashay over there and lift her skirt to see if she's wearin' pantaloons."

"That won't be necessary," laughed Jakes. "But on your way out, could you stop by and let her know I'm sittin' over here and would like to talk to her when she's got a minute?"

"Sure, but she keeps lookin' over this away, so she already knows you're here."

"Could be, Kid, but tell her anyway."

Chapter 7

Arriving a few minutes before six, the Alamo Kid led Jamison Jakes into the ornate waiting room of Doctor Benjamin Hopper. Being alone in the room, surrounded by dark wood-paneled walls, they had their choice of the large, leather-bound chairs. A chandelier hung from the center of the ceiling with a profusion of crystal bobbles encircling each large candle holder. Crushed velvet draperies, accenting leaded windows, reached to the floor. A thick rug from the Orient softened the expanse of oak flooring. Solid brass spittoons were placed beside each chair.

Before the out-of-place visitors were allowed to get too comfortable, a large woman in a white dress approached them from behind a high wooden counter.

"Which one of us is Mister Jakes?" inquired the lady, squinting at the watch pinned to her dress.

"Mister Jakes is the one a' us which can't see, lady," replied the Alamo Kid, with the sarcasm that was his trademark.

"I'm Jamison Jakes, ma'am," Jakes answered quickly. "I sure do hope the doctor's expectin' me."

"Indeed he is, Mister Jakes. And you need to appreciate that Doctor Hopper is giving up a very special meeting of the board of education to examine you this late in the day. He takes his civic responsibilities very seriously. Now, I need to collect some information from you before you meet with the doctor. Perhaps your friend can read the questions to you and write down the answers in the space provided."

"Uh, ma'am," Jakes stated hurriedly. "My friend fell off his horse and hurt the fingers on his writin' hand. I'm afraid he won't be any help."

The Alamo Kid gave Jamison Jakes a slight nudge of thanks.

"Oh, very well, I'll do it," she answered sharply. "I'll skip some of the less critical questions and we can fill those in later if the doctor thinks it's necessary."

The questions began.

"Full name?"

"Joshua Jamison Jakes."

"Age?"

"Thirty-four."

"What is the nature of our problem?"

"We are blind. I mean, I'm blind."

"Cause of the problem?"

"Pistol whipped on the head."

"Oh! Oh, dear me! Are you a sheriff or something like that?"

"No, ma'am, I'm just a cowboy who was in the wrong place."

"And what place was that, might I ask?"

"Right where that hombre was swingin' his pistol, ma'am."

At that moment, the door to the doctor's inner office opened and two men exited into the waiting room, interrupting the question-and-answer session.

"I'll see you again on Wednesday, Mike," a small man in a white coat said to the departing patient. "Keep putting those drops in your eyes until the bottle's all used up".

The little man's attention turned to the two sitting in front of the large woman.

"Ah, yes. Mister Alamo. So nice to see you again. And this must be your friend, Mister..."

"Jakes," offered the Alamo Kid. "Jamison Jakes."

"Yes, indeed. Mister Jakes. And what may we do for you?"

"I'd be much obliged if you could make me see again."

The doctor allowed the woman to go home for the evening before leading Jamison Jakes to the inner office, leaving the Alamo Kid alone in the waiting room. The Kid paced for awhile, but thinking perhaps his spurs were making too much noise, stopped in front of the stained-glass window. Rays of the setting sun were shining through the spectrum in front of him, washing pastel colors across his youthful face.

For reasons foreign to him, tears began to flow down his cheeks and he heard himself talking out loud in a shaky voice.

"Dear God, I don't know nothin' 'bout you, 'cept what I heard them circuit-ridin' preachers say when I was a little boy. But what they said has sorta stuck with me ever since. It was somethin' 'bout iffen we talk to you askin' fer things you can give us, then you prob'ly would. Especially iffen them things wasn't fer yerself.

"Well, sir, I'll tell you this right up front -- I don't want nothin' fer myself, 'cause I can take care a' me all I need. But ol' Jamison, he's gotta have a lotta help. You prob'ly saw him out there on the road when we was comin' down here, the way he almost killed hisself?

"Bein' able to see is mighty important to that man, God. And that makes it mighty important to me, too. So iffen you could do somethin' to help him, I'd be owin' you fer a good long spell. An' I promise you somethin': iffen you give him back his eyes, I won't go 'round tellin' lies like that Davy Crockett was my granddaddy, 'cause you and me both know he weren't. But, iffen it's all the same to you, I'd like to keep the 'Alamo Kid' handle."

In the examination room, Jamison Jakes was being subjected to all sorts of poking and rubbing and thumping, each followed by an "uh-huh" from the doctor.

Doctor Benjamin Hopper was a study in human contradictions. Small of stature but big in intelligence, he had chosen to give up a successful medical practice in Baltimore to start a new one in Denver. Greatly influenced by dime novels written by Ned Buntline, his hair and moustache had grown long to resemble a picture of Wild Bill Hickok he must have seen in a magazine. He did, in fact, appear to be Hickok in miniature. In spite of his wish to be seen as a rugged frontiersman, he could not quite abandon his New England breeding and Harvard education. This was apparent when he spoke. His sentences were textbook; his attempts at conversation, strained.

During the test to measure the extent of his vision, even Jakes was surprised at the amount of light he was able to discern and his ability to describe some of the shapes shown to him by the doctor. He was told to concentrate hard, looking only at each object presented.

At the end of the lengthy examination, the doctor applied a pungent-smelling salve to Jamison Jakes' healing head wound.

"Well, Mister Jakes," Hopper finally said, "I think we'll be able to do something for you. At least, I'd like to give it a try."

"Hey, that's great, Doc! Just give me the medicine and let me get started."

"No, it's a bit more complicated than that, I'm afraid. It will require an operation."

"Whoa, there, Doc. Whatta you mean? I was hopin' I

could get by without havin' to be cut open."

"You've got something called a subdural hemorrhage. That's a ten-dollar term for an injury to the head that breaks blood vessels. The blood, and other fluids attracted to the injury, put pressure on the brain. In your case, the pressure is affecting the optic nerve, which has the job of sending sight messages from the eyes to the brain. If this pressure is relieved, there's some chance that most of your vision will come back."

"None of that makes too much sense to me, Doc. The only thing I know 'bout operations is what I saw in the war, and I didn't like any of that. When they had me in a field hospital I saw lots of cuttin' and heard lots of screamin' from mighty tough men when they'd be getting' their arms or legs sawed off or their bellies sewed up. No sir, I don't even like the sound of the word 'operation'."

"We've come a long way since the war, Mister Jakes. There's a fine anesthesia called ether that's used every day now. It puts you sound asleep and you stay that way until the operation's over. They had ether during the war, but not nearly enough of it."

"What'll happen if you don't operate?"

"There's some chance that the condition will clear up by itself over time. There's also the possibility that the problem will get worse. If that's the case, other things will start to happen, like bad headaches, loss of balance, or maybe even paralysis in parts of your body."

"How would the operation work?" asked an increasingly anxious Jakes.

"We'll put you in the hospital for a few days before we operate. This is to build up your strength so you can recover faster. The procedure itself will be done in a room where everything is clean and sterile and my associate, Doctor Westland, will assist me with the surgery. It'll take quite a bit of time. We'll drill a small hole into your skull and this hole will allow the accumulated blood and fluid to drain away from your brain, which, in turn, will relieve the pressure on your optic nerve. Then over a period of days, we'll expose your eyes to more and more light until you're able to tolerate full sunlight again."

"Can I have some time to think about this, Doc?" Jamison Jakes' entire system was calling out for a big swig of whiskey.

"Sure, but you need to decide in the next day or two, and even if you decide against the operation, you should be placed in the hospital where you can get proper care for some of the other symptoms as they come along."

"Okay, Doc. I'll have the Kid let you know by noon tomorrow what I decide. Thanks for checkin' me out and tellin' me straight what it is I gotta do. How much do I owe you for your time? I want to settle up, so if I don't come back, we'll be even."

Walking back to the hotel, Jamison Jakes tried to explain to the Alamo Kid what the doctor had told him. The Kid understood even less than Jakes, but shared his concerns about the idea of surgery.

"I just don't know iffen I could do that myself, Preacher," the Kid offered, unreassuringly. "How you gonna know fer sure you can't feel the cuttin' an' the drillin' even though they give you that ether stuff? How you gonna know that maybe it just makes it so's you can't move or yell out or nothin', but can really feel it? No sir, I'd never let me be cut on."

"The doc wants know by tomorrow what I'm gonna do," said Jakes matter-of - factly. "Before I make up my mind, I wanna talk with Maryalice."

"The woman at the hotel? 'Bout what?"

"Not bein' able to see. You probably couldn't tell, because she can do so many things so well, but she's stone-cold blind."

"Holy shit," said an astonished Alamo Kid. "Why, she looks right at you all the time she's talkin' to you. How you

41

s'pose she's able to do that?"

"Practice, Kid. A lifetime of practice."

Jamison Jakes had downed almost a half bottle of corn whiskey before Maryalice was able to join him at his table in the café. The Kid had obliged Jakes' request to be alone with the dark-haired woman by joining a poker game. Among his other self-proclaimed talents, the Alamo Kid was "the best damn poker player west a' the Mississippi."

Maryalice sat quietly listening to Jakes refill his glass, then spoke in a scolding voice.

"Sounds to me like you're treating a mighty big thirst."

"A mighty big concern is a better way of puttin' it," Jakes responded grimly.

"What concern? The Kid told me things went very well with the doctor and you just need a simple operation before you can see again."

"A simple operation? He told you that?"

"Yes, he said it was so simple that he could have it done to him while he was standing up, but that you would probably need to have some kind of pain killer."

"That pompous little ass," Jakes smiled.

"I know it's not simple, Jamison. Tell me, when will you have it done? I'm so happy and excited for you!"

"I'm not sure I'm going to have it done, Maryalice. I'm just not sure at all." Jakes spoke as though the decision had already been made.

"Why in the world not?"

"Maybe it won't work. The doc told me that it might take care of itself without an operation so I may just wait and see if it'll clear up."

"And what if it doesn't? What then? How long will you wait to see if it'll cure itself? A week? A month? A year? Five, ten, twenty years? How long Jamison?"

"Well, no longer than a month."

"A month! A month without being able to see, just

because you're afraid! Oh, what a wasteful person you are, Jamison Jakes!" Maryalice paused for a moment to regain some composure, and then continued.

"What will you do for that month? I know what you'll do. You'll sit around drinking and feeling sorry for yourself and having people feel sorry for you. You'll hold the arm of the Alamo Kid while he leads you around. You'll wake up every morning praying to God that this is the morning the miracle happens and you'll be afraid to go to sleep at night because you can't face another disappointing morning. You won't bother to learn the hard lessons it takes to get along in a dark world because you'll think it's just a matter of time before you can see again. And the longer you wait, the more of a burden you'll become and the less likely you'll ever see again."

Maryalice's voice quivered with anger.

"But the worst part of waiting a month is that you won't be able to see during that time. Jamison, you're crazy for not wanting to try. If only I could see for that one month you're so stupidly willing to throw away! If God would grant me just thirty days of sight. To see a flower. A sunset. To see your face. Oh, please don't wait -- not another day. You let the doctor know first thing in the morning that you'll do it! Even if you die on the operating table, you will have died trying. Then I'll remember Jamison Jakes, the man, and not Jamison Jakes, the town's blind beggar! If I'd been given any hope to see, I would have done anything. You're being given a chance that few who are blind are ever given. You're such a fool. Please don't let this chance pass by."

For the second time in his life, a woman had called Jamison Jakes a fool. This time he thought he'd better listen.

Somewhere in the middle of the table, the fingers of Jamison Jakes met those of Maryalice Wheeler and intertwined for a brief moment before Jakes took the palm of her hand and pressed it softly against his lips.

Chapter 8

Doctor Hopper's office hadn't opened when Jamison Jakes and the Alamo Kid arrived early the next morning. After a half-hour of nervous waiting, the large woman in the white dress showed up and unlocked the door.

"Please be seated, gentlemen. The doctor will not be in this morning but he has left instructions for you to follow, Mister Jakes, in case you have decided to have the operation."

"Yes, ma'am, that's what I've decided to do."

"Very well. We are pleased with your decision. You should make arrangements with the hospital as soon as possible. Tell them you are Doctor Hopper's patient and they will admit you right away. He will come by as soon as possible and explain what is to happen next. The hospital is one block south of here."

"Thank you kindly, ma'am," Jamison Jakes said with a ring to his voice that had been missing for a long time. "We'll go right down to the hospital and get me a room. Let's get started!"

"Before you leave, we need to discuss the financial aspect of your treatment."

"You mean, how I'm gonna pay? Heck, ma'am, no problem there. We've still got almost all the money the people of Cheyenne gave us before we came down here."

"The doctor has left an estimate of the expenses. The total will approximate six-hundred and fifty dollars."

Jamison Jakes felt the bottom drop from his dream.

"Six-hundred and fifty dollars! We don't have near that much. We started out with somethin' over two hundred and we've been real careful not to spend any more than we really needed. But six-hundred and fifty dollars...", Jakes' voice trailed off to a softness that couldn't be heard.

"Well, ma'am," the Alamo Kid said after a tense moment of silence. "I reckon we'll just have to come back a bit later. Me an' the Preacher needs to put our heads together an' figger out how we's gonna come up with that kind a' money. You tell the sawbones it may take a couple days to raise it, but he can plan on doin' the job."

Out on the street, the Alamo Kid tried to repair Jakes' shattered spirit.

"I already got a plan worked out, Jamison. I'm gonna take what money we got left an' find me the biggest poker game goin' in the territory. I'll win us what we need in no time."

"Don't go silly on me, Kid. I appreciate what you're tryin' to do, but you don't play poker all that well."

"You don't know that! You ain't never seen me play. Once I won more'n three hundred dollars in less than ten hours a' playin'. I know I can do it. You gotta let me try. All we'll lose is the money we got, an' that ain't enough to do nothin' with no ways. We ain't gonna be no worse off iffen I lose, but iffen I win, you can have that operation. And I'm gonna win!"

"Okay, Kid," Jakes said with a sigh. "I don't know, but maybe what you say makes some sense. Just get me back to the hotel so Maryalice can tend to me while you head on out to strike it rich at the poker table."

Shortly after Jamison Jakes returned to the hotel café, he was joined by Maryalice.

"The Kid told me about the money you need. I know everything is going to work out, Jamison." She held his hand firmly between the two of hers. "Things have come along too well for anything to go wrong now."

"Maybe you're right, Maryalice. For the first time since my head got bashed, I'm startin' to believe I'll get my sight back. It's right here in my gut. I know I'm gonna see again."

"What will you do then? Where will you go? Back to working with cattle?"

"Nope. Me and the Kid got a plan. Soon as I'm able, and if the winter don't beat us, we'll be headin' out for the Idaho Panhandle to dig silver."

"Isn't gold supposed to be the thing that everyone's after? Why are you going looking for silver?"

"We don't care much for crowds. Anyway, most of the good gold's been found and it's made a lotta men rich. There's not too many out there lookin' for silver, so Idaho seems like the place to be for the next little while."

"Couldn't you just find a good paying job around here?" Maryalice asked hopefully. "Or you could look for silver in Ouray or Telluride, or even Silverton itself. Those places are a ways off, too, but you could get back here once in a while. If you go all the way to Idaho, you'll never get back to Denver."

"No reason to come back to Denver. Wouldn't be here now except this is where the doc is. I got to agree with the Kid, even though I've never seen the place, Denver's just too dang big. Nope, soon as I get my eyes back, I'm makin' tracks out of here."

Being blind at that moment spared Jamison Jakes the discomfort that he surely would have felt if he had seen the moisture on the tanned cheeks of Maryalice Wheeler.

"Excuse me for a while, Jamison; I have some things to do." Maryalice was able to speak without letting Jakes hear her anguish.

"Why, sure, pretty lady. I been takin' up too much of your time as it is."

It was sometime in the early morning hours when Jamison Jakes was awakened by the loud whoops and jangling Mexican spurs of a prancing Alamo Kid.

"Wake up, Preacher Man, wake up fer sure! I'm back an' I'm rich an' you're gonna have that operation! No question 'bout it! I don't rightly know how much I got 'cause I didn't take no time to count it after winnin' that last pot. But it was a fat one! Come on, Preacher, git up! I feel like dancin'!"

With that the Alamo Kid pulled Jamison Jakes to his feet and hugged him and made him waltz in circles until his head was spinning.

"Whoa, Kid, settle down," Jakes laughed. "Doc told me not to do much movin'. Besides, we don't wanna have to use all that money to pay a fine for disturbin' the peace!"

It took Jamison Jakes and the Alamo Kid some time to count the money using their own peculiar system. The Kid would identify the size of a gold piece and Jakes would take all the same- sized coins in his hands, count them, and tell the Alamo Kid what each pile was worth. When the counting was done, Jakes announced with a whistle, "Kid, we've got more than a thousand dollars here." Then reality hit. "A thousand dollars! Kid, you did it! You really did it! I'm gonna see again!"

Knowing it was useless to try to sleep the rest of the night, Jakes and the Kid made more detailed plans for going to Idaho as they waited for the Kid to say when it was light enough for them to head for the hospital.

Doctor Hopper admitted Jamison Jakes into the hospital, where he would rest for three days before the operation. During that time, Jakes was given food that was worse than he had ever tasted before, made to swallow pills designed for a bull, and was told when he could go to the bathroom. The doctor came to see him once a day and each time spewed out a lot of "uh-huhs." His parting remark was always the same, "Things are coming along very nicely. Very nicely, indeed."

The Alamo Kid visited many times each day as well, until he was caught trying to smuggle in a bottle of whiskey to share with Jakes and was unceremoniously tossed out by two large orderlies. This hurt the Kid's pride more than anything else, and he vowed to get even as soon as Jakes was discharged. He was too good a friend to blow holes through the hospital windows while Jamison Jakes was a patient.

Jakes wondered why Maryalice hadn't visited.

On the morning of the operation, Jakes was given some powders mixed in water to calm him, but the concoction did little to assuage his fears. He listened to talk between the doctor and his associate, but it meant nothing to him. He heard the clank and the clunk of the medical instruments, but he couldn't picture what they might look like. So, in his mind's eye, he conjured up a box filled with carpenter's tools: saws of different sizes, hammers and chisels, punch awls, and especially drills with huge bits that would soon be boring into his head.

Maybe because of these thoughts, or from natural reactions, Jakes began fighting the entire process. When the ether mask was placed on his face, he lashed out so suddenly and violently that the mask was knocked from the hand of the nurse holding it. Doctor Hopper's shout for help brought the sound of feet running into the room. Jakes felt his flailing arms being held down by many hands and the pressure of restraints being attached, first to his wrists, then to his feet and legs, and then across his body. His head was held in a vise-like human grip and he once again felt the mask on his face.

Hopper had told Jakes on the first attempt to count backward from fifty as the ether dripped. This time, the doctor considered the persistent cursing of Jamison Jakes to be sufficient inducement for breathing deeply.

As the ether did its job, Jakes' mind began to spin. Circles within circles of reds, blues, and yellows, first spiraling clockwise then reversing time and again until they ended in the pit of his stomach.

Tumbling end-over-end chasing the circles were the faces of his mother and father, of Dickie Hubbard and Hannah Robbins, and of the Alamo Kid. Finally, he saw what he thought must have been the likeness of Maryalice Wheeler.

He heard a rooster crow, and everything went black.

Jakes' recovery from surgery was terrible and included two days of ether-induced vomiting. He had no appetite. The mere mention of food sent his head into the bedpan. The pain from the drilled hole was excruciating. With his eyes tightly bandaged, he didn't know day from night, except that when the nurses woke him to give him pills, he figured it was night.

On the third day after the operation, the doctor said it was time to remove the bandages, but for just a few minutes. He came late at night so that he could remove the bandages from Jakes' eyes in complete darkness. Jakes was told to open his eyelids very slowly and to report if he felt any discomfort when his eyes were completely open.

Jamison Jakes' heart was pounding with both hope and fear as he felt the bandages being unwrapped from his head. He held his breath when the cotton balls covering his eyelids were gently taken away. He struggled to keep his eyes closed until he was given permission to open them.

"Now," said Hopper in a friendly voice, "I'm going to light

a match. When I tell you, open your eyes and let me know if you can see the flame.... All right, the match is lit. Very slowly, open your eyes."

"Dear Lord," Jakes prayed to himself, "please let me see that match."

Opening his eyes, Jakes blinked hard a few times before spotting the faint glow across the room.

"Doc, I can see it! I can see the light! Doc, I can see it, I really can! Yes, now you're making it do circles. Now up and down. Now crossways."

Hopper yelled "ouch" as the match burned its way to his fingers.

"Light another one, Doc. Let me look some more!"

"No, not tonight. We'll add a little more time each day. Too much too soon would defeat our purpose. The nurse will bandage your head and eyes again now. Tell me, was the match light in sharp focus?"

"Well, no, not real sharp. More like lookin' at a pool of water that just had a rock thrown in. A bit wavy and sort of fuzzy around the edges."

"That may clear up with time," said Dr. Hopper as he headed for the door. "The main thing is, you were able to see light and distinguish movement."

"Doc," Jamison Jakes said quietly. "God bless you, Doc. God bless you real good."

Over the next five days Hopper exposed Jakes' recovering eyes to more and more light until he was finally able to say, "Mister Jakes, we're ready to have you look out the window."

It was late in the evening and the sun was half-set in a purple sky. In the distance, lightening flashed in jagged bolts behind low-hanging clouds. The wind blew through the tree tops, sending autumn leaves swirling onto the street below as Denver's working people scurried through them trying to get home before the rain began.

Jakes saw it all. The sun, the lightening, the floating leaves, and the rushing people. It was like seeing for the first time. He drank it in like a parched river bed welcoming a cloudburst.

"Come, that's enough for now. Back to bed with you."

"Doc, I saw everything I looked at. But a lot of things are still fuzzy.

"Uh-huh," Hopper responded. "It may be that I'll have to fit you with a pair of spectacles. I'll sign you out of here tomorrow and you can come by my office for some seeing tests."

"Spectacles are for old folks. I'm not gonna wear those things."

"Mister. Jakes," Dr. Hopper said with a deep sigh, "those 'things' are also intended for people who want to see well."

The Alamo Kid was sitting on the hospital steps when Jamison Jakes came through the door. The Kid stood when he saw his friend and approached him with a broad grin. Jakes might not have recognized him except for the jangle of the Kid's spurs.

"Well, iffen you ain't a sight to behold!" said the Kid in a near shout. "Ain't that a wonderment? There you was a week ago, blind as a coot, havin' to be wet-nursed day and night. But just look at you now! Like a high-steppin' stallion rearin' fer a fight."

"Jesus, Kid, it's good to see you," said Jakes excitedly. He moved quickly toward the Kid and grabbed him in a bear hug. "And if it hadn't been for you and your poker luck, I would've stayed blind as a coot. I owe you, Kid, I sure enough do."

"Then turn me loose! Don't want folks a' thinkin' you've gone strange, do you?"

Walking toward the doctor's office, the two friends were quiet for a long while. Then the Kid asked, "Jamison, what was it like not bein' able to see?"

"It's really a bad, scary thing," came Jakes' pensive reply. "You can hear, and feel, and smell and talk. But you never know what's happenin' if you can't hear it or feel it or smell it. When you can't see, it's about as close to dyin' as I ever care to get."

"Out there on the trail, when you tried to put your gun in your mouth, would you a' done it, would you a' pulled the trigger iffen I hadn't a' been there?"

"No, Kid, I wouldn't. It was because you *were* there that I knew I could pull the stunt and be stopped."

"I'm a' feared to die, Jamison. Just flat out a' feared. I dream 'bout it a lot an' I wake up sweatin' an' sometimes yellin' an' once I dreamt I was in a river drownin' an' 'fore I could git myself awake, I pissed my bed."

"Everyone's afraid to die, Kid. I was afraid when they put me to sleep in the hospital that I wasn't gonna wake up. But everybody who ever lived will have to die sooner or later."

"Yeah, I know. But with me, it ain't gonna be from old age or the ague. When I go, it's gonna be 'cause someone's faster on the draw, an' that man ain't been born yet, so I guess I'll be 'round fer a long time."

"You still messin' with the idea of bein' a gun slinger?" Jakes asked with annoyance. "There's no reason you have to do that for a livin'. We're headed out to Idaho to make lots of money from the silver we're gonna dig."

"I won't be in it fer the money. I don't think takin' money fer gun fightin' is ever right. It ain't a job, it's somethin' else, somethin' I can't rightly 'splain."

"You don't have to explain to me, Kid," Jakes said in all sincerity. "I guess I'm just not the gambler you are. Every man to his own medicine, I always say. I just hope you don't run into anyone who's faster than you, that's all."

"So do I, Preacher man, so do I."

As the two companions were leaving Hopper's office after

Jakes' eye examination, Jakes said, "If I can see as good as I did when the doc put that seein' contraption on my face, I guess wearin' spectacles won't be too bad. I told him to make me up a couple of pairs in case one gets lost or broken when we're out on the trail."

"Hell, Jamison," said the Alamo Kid, "I bet you won't be wearin' 'em half the time once you git used to seein' the world through your real eyes. My pa wore specs, but he always took 'em off 'fore he laid it on me. Guess he was a' feared iffen I ever hit him back, they might get broke and it'd cost him money. Last thing I done after I hit him with that ax handle, 'fore I took off, was to stomp on his specs."

"Show me where the hotel is, Kid. I want to see Maryalice."

"I'm not sure that's somethin' you wanna be in a hurry to do, Preacher. She's fit to be tied here of late. When I was givin' her the message you sent her from the hospital, she all but took my head off. Yelled somethin' 'bout you bein' a coward, that you was tryin' to be a man but was lackin' the wherewithal to do it. She musta been eatin' on some chilies 'cause she sure had pepper on her tongue when I said your name. Never even let me give her the message."

"Then maybe I'll just go quietly into the hotel and not let her know I'm there. I sure don't want her mad at me and cause a ruckus. I wonder what the problem is. The last time we talked, just before I went to the hospital, she was real friendly. Fact is, if she hadn't talked to me the way she did, I might not've had the guts to have the operation. Beats me what burr she's got under her saddle."

"Pardon my sayin'," responded the Alamo Kid gently, "but you're sure one stupid jackass."

"How so?"

"The woman really likes you, Preacher. Only time a woman gits that mad at a man fer no good reason is that she really likes him. Once I had me a girl I was seein' regular. Met her at a Sunday sociable my ma was always dragin' me off to. Name was Janice Brock, an' she was a looker. Anyways, me and Janice went to a lot a parties an' things together an' always had a real good time. Then one day, outta the blue, and fer no good reason that I knowed, we was walkin' down the road after one of them sociables an' she was carryin' a glass a' lemonade in her hand an' she yells out, 'I hate you, Ellsworth Stipes!' an' she lets that glass fly an' missed my head by just barely. When I went home an' told Ma what happened, she just laughed an' said that was the way girls hadda sayin' they really like a boy.

"So I figger Maryalice yells when she hears your name 'cause she really likes you, but don't let on 'cause she don't want you to know."

"Ellsworth?" laughed Jamison Jakes. "Your name is Ellsworth? No wonder you wanna be called 'Alamo Kid.' Whoweee! Ellsworth!"

Maryalice wasn't at the hotel when the two arrived. The cook told Jakes that she started her shift at three o'clock. Jakes was surprised by what the cook looked like. He'd pictured the man as small and skinny, to match the high-pitched voice and slight lisp. Instead, the cook was large, with a beard at least a foot long.

"Sure is nice seein' you lookin' so good, Mister Jakes. Lot's a' folks was prayin' real hard that everythin' would be okay with the operation and all."

"I appreciate that, Cookie. I really do."

The Alamo Kid gave Jakes the key to the room and was off in search of a poker game. Jakes toyed for a moment with the idea of asking the clerk for Maryalice's room number and paying her a visit, but decided against it. He wasn't sure what her reaction might be but he knew he'd be braver in a public place. He shook his head trying to understand why she should be angry in the first place.

Maybe it would be easier to just leave town without seeing her.

In the room, he pulled off his boots, unbuckled his belt, and stretched out on the bed. Walking from the doctor's office had sapped his energy. A few hours of napping would get him back on his feet; then he would decide about Maryalice. He really did want to see her, even fuzzy in the distance. He was curious to know if he was as wrong about her looks as he had been about the cook's.

Chapter 9

It was dusk when Jamison Jakes was wakened by the jingle of the Alamo Kid's spurs coming down the hall. The door opened slowly, letting in a crack of light from the hallway.

"It's okay, Kid; I'm awake. Come on in."

"Won me a small pot, Jamison. Let's go down an' spend it on a side a' beef. Bet you ain't had a man's meal since you went to that hospital."

"You're sure right, Kid. Haven't had a drink of anythin' that burns either. How's about goin' down and bringin' us up a bottle of the good stuff."

"Hell no. You ain't gonna git liquored up here in the room. I ain't your nursemaid no more, no ways. You wanna bottle, go git it yourself." There was a serious tone in the Kid's voice, enough to let Jakes know he shouldn't press the issue.

"Kid, did you see Maryalice down there?"

"Sure, she's there. That's where she makes her livin'. She's there ever day."

"Does she know that I'm out of the hospital and back here

in the hotel?"

"How the hell do I know what she knows? Lotta people seen you today, an' you talked with the cook, askin' 'bout her. She must know by now. But iffen you're askin' did I tell her, the answer's no. You scared a' goin' down there? Is that why you was sendin' me, 'cause you're a' feared to face her?"

"I'm not afraid!" Jakes responded sharply. "What's there to be afraid of? She's just a woman, and a blind one at that. She can't hurt me. She couldn't even see me to hit me. I just don't know why she's so damned riled up. All we did was talk a few times. I don't remember ever sayin' anythin' out of line."

"I know," said the Kid in a more gentle tone. "They's two things I'll never understand 'til my dyin' day. One's the wonderment comin' from God an' the other's the wonderment comin' from women."

As a concession to his timid friend, the Alamo Kid agreed to have dinner in the hotel saloon rather than the café. Jakes assured the Kid that he would visit with Maryalice after he'd put a couple of drinks and a thick T-bone under his belt. The Kid was too hungry to argue the point.

They polished off a half-bottle of Platte River corn whiskey before their meal was served. The Alamo Kid finished his steak within minutes, took another quick shot of whiskey, and announced he was off to find some low-ante poker game down the street.

Jakes started to protest about being left alone, but thought better of it. By now the Platte River was flowing through his veins, bringing courage with it.

The saloon was filled with people from all walks of life, and Jakes sat quietly, looking from face to face. There were two men of means wearing store-bought suits and silk ties held down with gold stick pins. Three mountain men in crude handmade buckskins gathered at a corner table to talk trapping and trading. Store clerks with sleeve garters and bank tellers, some still wearing their green eye-shades, congregated to discuss daily commerce. Gamblers, some professional, some just feeling lucky, filled two tables and were being cared for and encouraged by saloon girls who knew that, regardless of who won at the tables, most of the money would be theirs by morning.

Jamison Jakes sipped his whiskey and promised himself that after one more drink he would look for Maryalice. His eyes were becoming more accustomed to the dim light. Studying each face along the bar, he was able to distinguish one from another without much trouble. One face in particular seemed unusual to him, yet somehow vaguely familiar. Jakes stood and moved closer to the bar for a better look. Within a few feet from the man, he could see the face clearly.

It was an old face, full of lines and crow's feet around the eyes from years of looking toward the sun. The long hair was gray and matched perfectly his drooping mustache.

"It's you!" yelled Jakes as he elbowed his way past the cowboy that stood between him and the old man.

Reaching the man who had been his Cheyenne guardian angel, Jakes yelled even more excitedly, "It's you! You're the man who saved my life! Everyone, listen up! This man saved my life in Cheyenne when I was 'bout to be gunned down. He shot two men dead in less than a second and saved my life, for sure!"

The old man did nothing more than raise his eyebrows, and his steel blue eyes looked directly into those of Jamison Jakes.

"Hush, boy."

"What you mean, hush? I want the whole world to know what you did for me."

"I said shut up, and I mean for you to shut up. I don't need any attention coming my way. Now, be quiet and leave me be."

"All right, mister. No harm meant. I just thought I'd never

run into you again, never be able to thank you for what you did. When I saw you standin' there, I was just so happy to see you that I couldn't be still, no matter what. Come over to my table and help me finish off my bottle."

"Seems to me you've had enough to drink. I'll sit with you a spell, if you like, but keep the cork in the bottle and a button on your mouth."

Back at the table, Jakes was full of questions:

"What's your name?"

"Where do you come from?"

"Why didn't you stay around Cheyenne after the shootin'?"

"What're you doin' in Denver?"

"How long will you be here?"

"Where're you off to next?"

"Whoa there, hold on a minute," the old man interrupted with a slight laugh. "I said I would sit a spell with you. I didn't know the price of admission was my life story."

"Aw, gee, I'm sorry, mister," said Jamison Jakes, sounding like an embarrassed child. "I'm just so glad to be able to thank you for what you did for me that I want to know all about you. Someday I'm gonna have grandchildren who'll wanna know the whole story of how I was saved from bein' killed, and I want 'em to know who they should be thankful to, 'cause if it wasn't for you, they never would've been. See what I mean?"

"I see that you're drunk. Maybe you should go to bed and sleep it off."

"Oh, sure, and when I wake up you'll be gone again and I'll never get to find out 'bout you. So, yeah, I'm a little drunk. That don't make me a bad person. You owe me some answers. Down home they say if a man saves another man's life, then the saver has to do whatever the saved person asks, 'cause... 'cause... Well, I don't remember the reasons why, but they're good ones."

"All right, boy," the old man said with a smile. "Far be it from me to disappoint your grandchildren. I'll tell you a little about me. Funny how nobody's ever been interested before."

With this, he reached for the bottle, pulled out the cork, and filled the glass in front of him. Jamison Jakes followed suit.

"As to who I am," he began, "name's Daniel True. I was born in the great state of Tennessee more years ago than I care to remember. I was a school teacher in a small college and a farmer when the war broke out. By the time I got back home, the school had closed and my farm had been stolen by carpetbaggers. I didn't have the spirit to stay around that little town, so I left there and tried my hand at cow-punching and then gambling; but I wasn't very good at either of those trades.

"Finally, about ten years ago, I became a hunter. Been making my living at that ever since. In Cheyenne, I was on a hunting trip. I'm here in Denver on another hunting trip. Tomorrow, I head back to Cheyenne, still hunting. Some folk say I'm the best hunter this side of the big river."

The old man paused to study Jakes' reaction. Getting none, he continued. "And I'm not about to argue with them."

"So what do you hunt?" Jakes asked, resting his heavy head in the palm of his hand. "You don't look like a buffalo man, or a trapper."

"I hunt men."

Jamison Jakes sat back in his chair so hard it almost tipped over.

"You mean, you're a bounty hunter?"

"Some people call me that. I like to think of myself as someone who can go where lawmen can't because of county lines or state lines, or because they just don't have the time, or inclination, to spend months, even years, looking for someone who should be in jail or on a gallows platform. I got nothing but time, and no reason to stay in one place. So I make my living going out and bringing back lawbreakers who shouldn't be running free in the first place."

"So when you were in Cheyenne...?"

"Yep, I was there on the trail of those hombres who were

robbing the hotel. I got wind they were heading for Cheyenne and got to town before they did. Never thought they'd try an early morning job, though."

"So you knew who they were! You didn't save my life 'cause I was gettin' killed. You saved my life so's you could collect the bounty."

"If that's the way you see it, then that's okay. But regardless of all you might be thinking, those men would have been in Cheyenne anyway, and you would have been in that hotel when they got there, and you would have tried to stop the robbery. The only thing different was, because I knew they were coming to Cheyenne, I was there too.

"And yes, I killed them and, yes, I collected five hundred dollars apiece for their carcasses. But you're alive today and talking about having grandchildren because I was there planting lead in them before they sent you to Boot Hill."

Jamison Jakes was about to offer another drunken apology when he felt a hand on his shoulder. He looked up through eyes made weak by injury and hazy from hours of drinking Platte River. He saw the face of a woman looking blankly toward him.

"Jamison?" asked the woman. "Is that you, Jamison Jakes? It's me, Maryalice."

Jakes froze at the sound of her voice. He really had intended to seek her out for a talk. He'd practiced many times in his head the things he would say to her, to discuss the confusion he was feeling, and to find out what he had done to upset her. But now all of this was spoiled. His big chance to be the one to initiate a discussion had been stolen.

So he did the only thing a man can do when he's been outdone by a woman. He got angry.

"What the hell you want, woman? Can't you see I'm tryin' to have a visit with my friend here? Go on about your chores. I'll come see you later!"

"Don't bother. I can tell you've been visiting with your

61

friend, the bottle, far too long as it is. If I can't talk to you sober, then I don't want to talk at all!"

The small lady turned abruptly and in her rush to flee her embarrassment, ran into a mountain man standing behind her.

"Hold on there, Missy," said the buckskin-clad man. "I don't dance with no woman I ain't been properly introduced to. My name's Luke and I already know who you are, so now that we've got that out of the way, let's dance!"

"No thank you," sobbed Maryalice. "I don't care to dance. I have to get back to work. Please! Leave me alone!"

"Aw, sure honey. I'll leave you alone as soon as you make me happy. If you ain't got time to dance, then how's 'bout a little kiss?" The trapper held the frightened girl roughly in his arms, trying to kiss her.

"Help me! Please, somebody help me!" There was fear in Maryalice's voice.

In a staggering flash, Jamison Jakes was at her side, yelling at the mountain man, "Turn her loose! You got no call to treat her that way! Turn her loose!"

Jakes grabbed the man by the shoulder and spun him around, only to be met by the full force of Luke's giant fist against his jaw. Jamison Jakes fell to the floor like a piece of cut timber.

Feeling a new sense of power, the huge man once again turned his attention to the girl.

"Okay, little honey, let's get on with the party. Unless, of course, theys other heroes 'round here wantin' to look after you." Luke began turning Maryalice around and around like he was spinning a top.

"Please don't do this to me! Please don't!" The exhausted young woman had expended all her energy fighting off the man.

"That's enough!" Daniel True stood and faced the man-bear.

"What's that, old timer?" Luke held on tightly to

Maryalice as he snarled at the gray-haired man standing in front of him.

"I said, that's enough. Party's over. Leave her be. You've scared the poor girl half out of her wits."

"And what if I don't care to leave her be?"

"Oh, nothing too bad," replied True as he slowly drew one of his wooden-handled Colts. "I figure a piece of lead in both your kneecaps will slow you down considerably."

For a moment the mountain man looked as though he might challenge the bounty hunter, but thought better of it as True cocked the hammer and pointed the pistol at Luke's knee.

"Aw, what the hell. Anyways, she's too skinny for my taste. I like some meat on my women."

With this, the predator released the woman and quickly left the saloon. Daniel True helped Maryalice to a chair and placed a glass of water into her trembling hands. She sipped the water between sobs.

"Where's Jamison?" Maryalice asked quietly once she was composed. "Is he all right?"

"He seems to be fine," answered the old man, seeing the once-unconscious form of Jamison Jakes begin to stir. "He seems to be just fine."

When Jakes woke up, he was in bed. His mouth hurt when he tried to open it and it felt like a tooth had broken off in his jaw. The top of his head was exploding from the afterglow of his trip down Platte River. With his first moan of the new day, he heard a movement next to his bed and realized the Alamo Kid was on the floor, trying to sleep.

Jakes struggled to piece together the events of the evening and how he had ended up in bed. He remembered eating...drinking...talking with someone about something very important. Yes, Daniel True. He remembered talking with Daniel True.

It hurt just trying to think.

There was a girl. What about the girl? She was in trouble. What kind of trouble? What girl? What kind of trouble was the girl in? Maryalice! It was Maryalice! What kind of trouble was Maryalice in? A fight. There was a fight with someone. Who fought? Why? Maryalice! The fight was about Maryalice. Someone was trying to hurt Maryalice.

"Maryalice!" Jakes sat up fast in his bed as he shouted her name. Pain shot through his left eyeball.

The Alamo Kid leaped from his blanket on the floor and instinctively reached for his gun, strapped outside the longjohns he slept in.

"Who's there?" the Kid cried out, trying to see in the dim morning light.

"Hold on, Kid! Don't shoot! It's me, Jamison."

"What the hell you screamin' 'bout? I coulda turned you into buzzard food."

"Sorry, Kid. I just remembered that Maryalice was being hurt."

"Musta been dreamin', Preacher. She looked okay to me when I come in last night. She was in the café after closin' time, drinkin' coffee with some old gray-headed man."

"Did you bring me up here to bed?"

"Hell no. You was on the bed, sleepin' like a baby, when I got here. I looked fer you in the saloon an' when I couldn't find you, I come on up. I was lookin' to borrow a few silvers to keep me in the game down at the Bird's Nest, but I couldn't even rouse you with a good shake; so I gived up and turned in. Musta been some night you had."

"I don't know, Kid. To tell the truth, I can't recall much of anything after you left the saloon. I know I talked to a man I knew once, the guy who saved my life up in Cheyenne. Then I was in a fight. From the way I'm hurtin', I lost the fight. Then, next I knew, I was here in the room, worryin' about Maryalice."

"That's what my Pa use to do, or at least, said he done."

The Alamo Kid had sadness in his voice. "At night, he'd beat the pudding' outta me an' Ma, an' in the morning' he'd swear he couldn't 'member a thing 'bout it. You're the only other person I ever knowed to use that excuse."

"It's not an excuse, Kid. For the life of me, I can't remember any more about last night than I just told you. I want to remember, but I can't."

"Then I don't know whether I wanna be like you, or feel real sorry fer you. See, I can 'member everythin' I done last night: the drinks I had, the food I ate, who I talked to, an' 'specially the bad cards I was holdin'. Sure would be nice iffen I could say I was playin' bad 'cause I had me a blank mind 'sted a' havin' to admit I was just playin' bad. Yessir, sometimes I'd rather be knowed as a drunk than a fool."

"Now who's the preacher?" asked Jakes, somewhat annoyed. "My head aches, my jaw feels busted, and I have to piss real bad. I don't want to pretend that I always do things exactly right, and I won't try to tell you that sometimes I don't drink too much. But I only get drunk when I have a good reason. I don't do it much, but I always have a good reason."

Having finished his defense, Jamison Jakes stood in the corner with the slop jar and relieved himself. Turning around, he started to make another comment on the subject of drinking, but thought better of it when he saw the Alamo Kid had returned to his blanket on the floor with his face to the wall. Sounds of sleep were coming from his open mouth. He may have been faking, but either way, Jakes knew his friend had finished talking for a while.

Thinking a ride in the cool morning air would be good for his system, Jakes quietly got into his clothes, strapped on his holster and reached for his hat. At that moment he saw his reflection in the cracked mirror that hung on the wall above the dresser.

"My Lord," he uttered. "I look like somethin' that should have the good sense to be dead."

He moved closer to the mirror to make sure there was no one standing beside him. Nope, it was his own face all right. He watched his hand outline the swelling that ran in a large oval from the line of his jaw to above his left eye. Both eyes were bloodshot and the corners were caked with dried mucous. He opened his mouth as far as the pain would allow and stuck his finger inside to locate the throbbing tooth. It was loose, but not broken. One thing to be thankful for at least.

The brisk morning air met Jakes full in the face as he stepped through the hotel doorway onto the boardwalk. He sucked in a deep breath, pulled his bandanna over his mouth and turned away from the wind to walk east toward the livery stable. It would be good to see his horse again and to feel a saddle between his legs for the first time in what seemed a century.

Nearing the livery, Jakes could see a light from a lantern flickering through the partially opened door, and as he got closer, he heard the muffled sound of low talking and the stomping of horses' hooves. Could it be horse thieves? He slowly drew his Colt from its holster and crept silently forward. It looked like one man, saddling a horse. But whose horse? And for that matter, whose saddle?

The click coming from Jamison Jakes' pistol cocking caused the man to freeze.

"Who are you and what are you doin' here?" Jakes demanded to know.

"Name's True, and I'm saddling my horse. Who wants to know? Step out where you can be seen." True's voice was gruff and irritable.

"Oh, Mister True," said Jakes, reholstering his .45. "Sorry, I didn't recognize you in the dim light."

"I'm surprised you recognize me at all," responded Daniel True sarcastically. "I'm surprised you even remember meeting me last night."

"I'd rather not think about last night." Jakes rubbed his

aching jaw.

"I guess there are days a man would just as soon forget. Had a few of those myself. What brings you out so early, boy?"

"Just thought a ride in the cold mornin' air might clear some cobwebs. Got some thinkin' to do as well. Always do my best thinkin' on horseback. Where you headed?"

"Same place I told you last night. Cheyenne."

"Yeah, I remember now," said Jakes with an almost-smile that hurt his split lip. "Headed back to Cheyenne on another huntin' trip. Who you after?"

"I'm looking for three different hombres. Whichever one I catch up to first will be the one I'm after. But I'd rather bag the one that's worth the most."

"Who might that be?" Jakes asked with a growing curiosity.

"Name's Emory Gordon. Bad medicine. Folks call him the 'Widowmaker' because of all the men he's killed. Seven at last count."

Daniel True reached into his saddlebag and pulled out a piece of rolled up paper.

"Here's a picture drawing of him. Ever see him around these parts?"

Jamison Jakes took the poster and studied the face. He noticed the reward offered was five-thousand dollars.

"Nope, he don't look familiar to me. Course, I haven't been seein' too good lately."

"Well, never mind. I'll find him if he's to be found. Something in my bones tells me he's heading for Cheyenne."

"What about the other two?"

"Pretty small apples by comparison. Somebody robbed the bank up in Thornton a few weeks ago. Didn't get much, just grabbed what he could carry in one hand. He's only worth fifty. The other's a renegade Indian named Nerak who's been leading a small band of young bucks, killing cattle and carrying off what they can load on pack animals. Cattlemen's Association put a thousand-dollar price tag on his head."

"Sound like you got a job of work cut out for you." There was a note of admiration in Jamison Jakes' voice.

"You're right about that, boy. And I'm already late getting to it. So just back off and I'll be on my way."

"Mind if I ride with you a ways?" Jakes asked.

"Not if you get a move on. I'd hoped to be two miles out by now."

"Be right with you, soon's I find my saddle."

The two men said nothing more until they reached the outskirts of Denver. Daniel True spoke first. "Looks like an early winter. Hope I get across the pass before the snow hits."

"What way you takin'?" asked Jakes.

"Nothing fancy. Plan to just stick to the stage road. Then if I get sick or have Indian trouble or tire out from sleeping on the ground, I'll know there's a relay station not far ahead."

This exchange was followed by another ten minutes of silence. Again, it was True who spoke.

"Had a nice chat with your woman last night after I carried you off to bed."

"My woman?" asked Jamison Jakes. "I don't have a woman."

"You know. That blind girl whose honor you were protecting when the mountain man got fresh with her. Surely you remember him; he's the one who sent you to bed early." Daniel True chuckled at his little joke.

"Oh, I know the woman you're talkin' about. I just don't consider her to be my woman, that's all.

"Well, I think she's hoping she might be someday," said Daniel True in a more serious tone. "But for the life of me I can't figure out why."

"What do you mean by that?"

"She could do a whole lot better, boy. A whole lot better."

Jakes wanted to argue the point, but couldn't think of an

anything strong enough to counter the charge. The two rode on in silence.

"I had a woman once." Again it was Daniel True who spoke. "Her name was Elizabeth. Just a small bit of humanity, she was. Lord, I loved that woman. I still dream about her when times are hard and I need a good dream. She comes walking up to me with sunlight shining through her hair, and she'll look at me and say, 'It's all right, Daniel, everything is all right' and then I wake up, and everything *is* all right, just like she said it would be."

"Was she your wife?" asked Jamison Jakes.

"No, just a sweetheart. She was half my age. Her pa and I taught literature and poetry in the same little college and I watched her grow up. He never approved of the arrangement when I started courting Elizabeth and it almost caused bad blood between him and me. Then I went off to do what I could in the war, and when I got back three years later, her pa told me she had married and was living up North, somewhere in Indiana."

"Did you go lookin' for her?"

"No. I thought about it for a long while. I told myself it was her pa who made her get married and if I could find her I could win her back and we would work things out. But then I reasoned that if she was happy with a husband and family, I had no business getting in the way."

"That's a sad tale, Mister True. A real sad tale."

"I guess it is. May be the same for you someday, if you turn your head to what's happening there in Denver. She's a fine woman."

"You mean Maryalice?"

"Good Lord, boy! You're dumber than a rock. Of course I mean Maryalice. Do you know any other women in Denver?"

"Well, no," Jakes admitted. "But I don't really know her, either. She was kind to me when I was laid up blind. We talked some, but never got on to anythin' serious."

"Well, take it from a man who's staked his life on outguessing the other person. There's more to her thinking than friendship. What I'm saying to you is, don't let her get away if you have any feelings for her at all. People being alone in this world isn't what God had in mind."

It was midmorning when Jamison Jakes and Daniel True said their goodbyes. Jakes walked around for a while, stretching his legs and watching his new friend ride over the hill and out of sight. For a moment he thought about riding after him, joining him on his hunting trip to Cheyenne, but he remembered there were things in Denver that were important to him. The Alamo Kid couldn't be left behind without an explanation. He needed to pick up his spectacles as soon as they were made. And, of course, there was Maryalice. What about Maryalice?

Chapter 10

It was a slow ride back to Denver. Jamison Jakes was lost in thought about himself, his life, past and present, and what the future might hold. He stopped and let his horse drink from a stream that came rushing in a torrent from somewhere unknown.

As he rested his tender buttocks, he reached into the worn saddlebag and found the stub of a pencil and a crumpled piece of paper. Using the smooth bark of an aspen tree for support, he wrote, "October 11, 1879. What?"

"What?" was a question he was asking himself. What will happen from this day on? This was a way of marking time – these dated, terse notes. Sometime in the future he would come across one of these papers stuffed somewhere in the clutter of his saddlebag and evaluate the happenings in his life between the recorded date and the time of the paper's rediscovery. Then he would have the answer to "What?" At least for that period of time.

This had been a standing habit of Jamison Jakes' since he

had learned to write. He would jot down a message to himself, sometimes listing a few details of the current situation and then compare that note with what had happened in his life from that point to the time he again found the message.

He had wrapped in a piece of oil cloth his grade-report, written on a slip of paper that his mother had given him after his first year of studies in his home-school, and had buried it behind their house in Kentucky with a promise to himself that someday he would dig it up. He was still a schoolboy when he left to join the war, and by the time he had returned, his boyhood promise had been forgotten. Somewhere, in the warm Kentucky ground, perhaps not far from the final resting place of his family, the academic history of Jamison Jakes' success in the first grade also lay buried.

Jakes was lost in melancholy reverie when his horse ambled into Denver. He stopped at the edge of town to have his first drink of the day. He wondered how many saloons he could find before he reached his hotel. He found seven, and had a drink in three.

The afternoon reached almost six o'clock when Jakes finally arrived at the hotel. The Alamo Kid wasn't in the room. Jakes realized the enormous hunger pangs he was experiencing came from twenty-four hours without food.

"Well," he thought, "guess I'll go to the café and have myself a steak; if Maryalice is there, I'll say howdy to her at the same time."

Jamison Jakes stood in front of the mirror to brush off some of the dust from the ride, looked at his reflection, smiled slightly, gave himself a thumbs up and left the room.

The café was almost filled when Jakes arrived. He found a small table in the corner of the room and uncorked the bottle he had brought with him from the adjoining saloon. He was beginning to feel warm and invincible, remembering the time in the war when he had been shot and two soldiers, one on each side of him, fell and didn't get up. They died and he lived. He drank a toast to the two men.

"Jamison."

There it was again. That voice.

"Jamison Jakes, is that you?"

"Yes, Maryalice. It's me."

"May I sit with you for a minute?"

"Sure. Are you all right? I mean, last night. Are you all right from last night?"

"Yes, I'm fine. Thank you for coming to my defense."

"Ha, a lot of defendin' I did. Mister True's the man to thank."

"I did thank him. But you were the first to help. Jamison, could we meet after I get off work and talk for a while?"

"Sure, that'll be okay, I guess. Do you want me to wait here?"

"It'll be a couple of hours. Could you come to my room after nine o'clock? Room 104."

"Okay. Room 104. Little after nine. See you then."

Jakes ate his dinner, trying not to think what might be in store for him at nine o'clock. Halfway through his T-bone, he corked the bottle, deciding he should be mostly sober when the two of them met.

At a few minutes past nine, Jakes stood at the door of Room 104. He knocked lightly, hoping maybe he wouldn't be heard.

"Come in, Jamison." Maryalice's voice was strong and determined.

His hand trembled as he grasped the door knob and slowly turned it. Once inside, he could smell the fragrance of lilac. The room was dark.

"Where are you?"

"Oh, I'm sorry, Jamison. I forgot to light the lamp. Could you do it?"

"Sure can," Jakes responded, reaching in his pocket for a

match. He struck it on the backside of his jeans, quickly found the lamp on the bedside table, and lit it.

"Sorry," she said again. "I don't have company very often."

He was about to respond when he caught sight of Maryalice. She was wearing a red dress that almost touched the floor, calling attention to her shiny black shoes. Her long dark hair fell in cascades on the front of her shoulders, reaching to her waist. Her hand clutched a long-stemmed red rose that was all but lost in the background of her dress. Her eyes were misty and Jakes wondered if she had been crying.

"Make yourself comfortable, Jamison. Can I offer you a drink?"

"Yes, please. I need a drink."

Maryalice moved with grace across the floor to the dresser, uncorked the new bottle, picked up a glass, poured the drink, moved toward Jakes, and stretched out her hand to meet his.

"Will you join me?"

"No, thank you."

"Don't you drink?"

"Yes, sometimes, but I'd rather not drink just now."

"Well, if it's all the same, I really need one."

"Why?"

"Why, what?"

"Why do you feel you need a drink? It's plain you've already had quite a few."

"I don't know. I can't explain it. I just get tied up in knots when I'm around you. I've started to dream about you at night and to think about you most of the day. And then I come here to talk to you and the room smells so nice and you look so pretty and I get mixed up in my head and I don't know what I'm supposed to do or how I'm supposed to act."

"Tell me what you remember about being blind," Maryalice asked gently.

"I try not to think about it. Those were real bad days."

"Do you remember how you were treated?"

"Yes, people were very kind to me."

"More kind than when you could see?"

"Sure, a lot more."

"Why do you suppose that was?"

"I guess they felt sorry for me."

"Yes, people do feel sorry for the blind. They're glad the blindness happened to someone else rather than them, so they show compassion out of gratitude." There was bitterness in her voice.

Jamison Jakes sat on the edge of the bed and downed his drink.

Maryalice continued, "But then it goes farther than compassion, or even pity. After a while, people become afraid, afraid to get too close or too friendly. Almost as if they're afraid they'll catch some blinding disease if they stay around you too long. Oh, everyone's nice enough, but they're afraid. Especially the men. Big, strong men turn into frightened little boys when I go near them, thinking I might touch them and some demon will posses them."

"Why, that's plain silliness. What makes you think anything like that goes on?"

"Living with it every day, that's how I know. Years of trying to talk with people in the café, or at church or on the street, or anywhere, and have them politely excuse themselves after just a few words. That's how I know. My talk with Mister True last night was the most I've ever talked with a man, other than you, since my father passed away. I get so hungry to talk about real things; things that matter. I want to hear what's been written in the latest books. I want someone to tell me about a beautiful sunset or describe a rainbow; otherwise, I'll forget those things and the day will come when my mind goes blank and all I'll do is shuffle around and pray to die because I can't remember anything but blackness."

Maryalice began to sob.

Jakes rose from the bed and held her in his arms.

"Hey," he said softly. "I'm not afraid of you because you're blind."

"I know that, but it's only because you've been there yourself. You know nothing evil happens to a person when they lose their sight. You know that no demon possesses your body. You know that all your feelings inside stay the same."

"I do know that for a fact, Maryalice. I surely do."

Jamison Jakes ran his fingers through the long, dark hair of the sobbing girl he held in his arms. In a short while her sobbing turned to sniffles and she rested her head on his chest.

"Remember that first day you came to town, Jamison, and I helped you with your bath?"

"Oh, lady, do I ever," Jakes chuckled.

"That was the first time I had ever touched a naked man. It felt so good to me. There hasn't been an hour go by since that day that I haven't thought about how it made me feel."

Beads of sweat covered his forehead.

"I've never had a lover, Jamison. Will you be my lover tonight?"

It was almost morning before Maryalice spoke again.

"Jamison, are you awake?"

"Yes."

"It was beautiful, Jamison. So very beautiful. It was like seeing a heaven full of beautiful stars and I was all warm and happy inside. Then I saw a rainbow, just like when I was a little girl. No one had to describe it to me, it was just there. Maybe next time, I can see a sunset, too."

"I hope I didn't hurt you," Jakes said. "It's been a long time since I was with a woman."

The first light of morning shone through the lace curtain and danced on the wall. The two bodies slowly untwined and turned in opposite directions. A dog barked in the distance and the sound of horse's hooves clopped along the street below.

The wagon the horse was pulling needed grease on its wheels.

"I love you, Jamison Jakes."

In a short while Maryalice was sleeping peacefully. Jakes closed his eyes for a few minutes, but his mind wouldn't let him sleep. He stared at the ceiling for a long while, then got up and quickly dressed. Before slipping from the room, he lightly touched the raven hair of the sleeping woman. "Goodbye," he whispered. "Goodbye, beautiful lady."

Jamison Jakes found the Alamo Kid asleep on the floor of the room they shared and was met with some irritation when he roused the Kid.

"What the hell you want now?"

"Kid, I'm leavin' town and there's a couple of things I'd like you to do."

"Leavin'? You mean now? This minute?"

"Yes, right now. But I need for you to stay around until Doctor Hopper has my spectacles ready. Then ride after me on the stage route to Cheyenne. I'll take my time so it'll be easy to catch up. Will you do that for me, Kid?"

"Yeah, I reckon. But why're you in such an all-fired hurry to git outta town? Did you steal somethin' and you're a' feared a' gittin' caught?"

"That's about right, Kid. That's just about right."

Chapter 11

Jamison Jakes pushed his horse hard for a full hour, trying to put as much distance as possible between him and Denver. When he realized that if he got too far along the stage road the Alamo Kid would have difficulty catching up, he slowed his pace.

He stopped before noon to make camp for the day, but the hard-blowing cold October wind stung his fingers so much he couldn't strike a match to light the campfire. He decided to press on to the stage relay station and lay up there until the Kid came along. At least it would be warm.

Snowflakes swirled through the air as Jakes leaned forward in his saddle, bending low to buffer the whistling wind.

"Damn," he said aloud, "I sure hope the winter keeps its pants on." He reached into the saddle bag and pulled out a bottle. "At least I can get my innards warm." He took a long swig and placed the bottle inside his mackinaw.

In the quiet of the afternoon, with no sound other than the steady cadence of his horse, he thought of Maryalice. She would be working by now, moving gracefully among the tables in the café. I wonder if she knows I've left town? Surely she must. If nothing else, the Alamo Kid would have gone to the café for a meal and told her. Good old Kid. He'll take care of it. Maybe I should have told him the whole story.

Much of Jakes' life had been lived with "maybes" and "what-ifs." He took another long swallow of whiskey.

It was almost dark when Jakes finally saw smoke rising from the chimney of a small building and knew the relay station had a fire going. In a few minutes he was inside, rubbing his hands vigorously in front of a potbellied stove. He was helping himself to a cup of steaming coffee when the back door opened.

"Well, howdy-do, mister. I didn't expect more company today. Folks call me Pappy. I run this here station. I was out back feedin' the horses. Who might you be?"

"Name's Jakes. Pleased to meet you, Pappy. Mind if I hang around here for a day or two until my partner catches up?"

"Nosiree, don't mind a bit. Not many humans around here this time of year. Stagecoach only runs once a week in the winter time. You headed north or south?"

"North. Hope to make Cheyenne before too many days. Got any plans for supper?"

"You bet I do," Pappy said with a broad grin. "Another feller been here since yesterday. Horse throwed a shoe and he's waitin' 'til the company's circuit ridin' blacksmith gets here so's he can get a new one made. He went to the woods a hour ago on foot to find some meat. Said if he's gonna eat here, he wanted to bring somethin' to the table. Whatever he brings back, we'll eat. If he don't have no luck, we'll have smoked ham. Got lots of smoked ham. And we'll have biscuits and some gravy. How's that sound?"

"Just like I've died and gone to heaven, Pappy."

Jamison Jakes took his horse to the barn, put her in the

only vacant stall, gave her a big scoop of grain, and covered her with a blanket.

"Better enjoy this good life while you can old girl. This may be the last warm night we'll have for quite a time."

Back in the cabin, Jakes hung up his mackinaw and pulled off his boots. He poured himself a half-cup of fresh coffee and finished filling the cup with whiskey from one of the two bottles he'd unwrapped from his bed roll.

"You provide the grub, Pappy," Jakes said as he put his feet on a chair in front of the stove, "and I'll provide the drinks."

"Seems like a fair trade to me, Jamison. Yes siree, seems more than fair."

Pappy began to share with Jakes all the reasons he was sure the winter would be a hard one when the door flew open wide, aided by a gust of wind. In the doorway stood a man swinging two rabbits above his head with one hand and holding a rifle in the other. One bandanna covered his face and nose, and another, covering his ears, was tied under his chin.

"Well, for God's sake! Look who's here!" a voice shouted through the bandanna. "What are you doing this far from Denver, boy?"

"Mister True, is that you under there?" Jamison Jakes almost spilled his coffee in his haste to get to his feet.

"It's me all right. How about skinning these rabbits while I get some heat into these old bones."

Before long, the three men were feasting on fried rabbit, sourdough biscuits covered with gravy, boiled turnips from Pappy's root cellar, and hot coffee laced with Platte River whiskey.

At the end of the meal, as Pappy busied himself cleaning up the dishes, Daniel True said, "I'm glad to see you again, boy. I enjoyed the little talk we had yesterday. You're an easy person to know."

"Same here, Daniel. Is there any chance we might ride

together to Cheyenne?"

"I don't know about that," True responded, rubbing his chin. "In my line of work, you do a lot better if you ride alone. But maybe the two of us would do okay."

"I'm afraid there would be three of us. See, I'm here waitin' for my friend to catch up so we can head out to Idaho and dig silver. He's a real good kid and wouldn't be any trouble at all."

"I'll sure have to think on that a while," Daniel True said with a shake of his head. "I've never teamed up with even one man before, let alone two."

"We could help you with your huntin'. You know, sorta like hound dogs. None of those hombres you're lookin' for know either me or the Kid. We could do a lot of sniffin' around, then you could move in and bag 'em."

"Interesting idea. Something like that might work. And not knowing how tough it's going to be getting across the pass, we might be of some help to each other."

"It's settled then," Jamison Jakes said with a smile. "The hunter just got himself a couple of bloodhounds."

By noon the next day, the company blacksmith had shown up and within the hour had replaced the thrown shoe on Daniel True's horse. The weather had cleared a bit and True was eager to hit the trail.

"You got a choice to make," he told Jakes. "Either ride with me now and have your friend catch up if he can, or wait for him here and the two of you find me later."

"It's easier for one man to catch up than two," Jakes reasoned, "so I'll go along with you."

The two men said their goodbyes to Pappy, and Jakes left instructions for the Alamo Kid to double-time after them as soon as he got to the relay station. Pappy promised to send him right along, especially since Pappy had the blacksmith to visit with for a few days.

On the trail, the two men seemed content to canter side by side for a long while. When they stopped to water their horses in a cold, crystal-clear stream, Daniel True finally spoke.

"This is my last hunt, Jamison. After I collect the bounty on the Widowmaker, I'm hanging up my guns."

"I'm glad to hear that, Daniel. Your kind of huntin' can be mighty dangerous. What'll you do?"

"I'll be heading back east. I've got a real hankering to go to Indiana."

There was an air of sadness in Daniel True's voice.

"I'm getting on in years, Jamison. My life's about run its course. Before my luck goes sour, I have to find out what happened to Elizabeth. It'll be enough just to stand on the street and watch her walk by. Just look at her, even if I don't speak. Who knows, she could be single again by now. If there's any chance in God's good mercy of us having a few years together, then I've got to make that happen."

"I admire you for that, Daniel. What made you decide all the sudden that's what you wanted to do?"

"It's not really all that sudden. I've thought on it for a lot of years. It just never seemed right before. It wasn't like I had a claim on her. She was so young when we fell in love. She had every right to change her mind about me and marry someone else. No woman should be expected to wait for a man as long as I needed her to wait for me."

"What if you get back there and find out she's passed away?" the practical side of Jamison Jakes asked.

"Then I'll find her grave and take her flowers and visit with her every day until I can go be with her on the other side."

Jakes began to see an entirely different Daniel True. Who was this man, this bounty hunter, this hired gun with the long gray hair and drooping moustache? What was really going on behind that craggy face and those sad blue eyes? Jakes found himself wishing he could experience some of those strong, yet tender, feelings the old man was expressing without effort.

"You never married?" Jakes asked.

"Nope. Never was in one place long enough to get to know a woman real good. Wouldn't have been fair, anyway. Elizabeth would have been in the way. I can't explain it, boy. It may not be natural, the way I feel about her. I waited half my life for her to come along. Then she was gone. Don't try to understand it."

"You never even bedded down with any women?" Jamison Jakes' tone was skeptical.

"Oh, I did my share of that, I guess. But I always felt bad about it afterward."

"How do you mean?"

"On the one hand, I felt like I was being unfaithful to Elizabeth. On the other, I was never honest with the woman I was with because, in my mind's eye, whoever she was, she was always Elizabeth."

Jamison Jakes didn't ask any more questions. The two men tightened the cinches on their saddles, mounted, and headed north once again. He stayed a few yards behind Daniel True as they rode in the center of the road, between the ruts that the years of stagecoach runs had cut. He was feeling some embarrassment about the discussion that had just ended.

It was almost dark when the two travelers pulled off the road and set up camp. Daniel True offered to go hunt some meat for supper while Jakes built the campfire. Within ten minutes the loud report of a rifle echoed through the brisk air, and soon Daniel True rode into camp with a young antelope slung over his horse's neck in front of the saddle horn.

"I'll swear, Daniel," Jakes said, "you hardly gave me enough time to get the fire going."

"Sorry, but I ran into a whole herd of these fellows on their way down to lower ground for the winter. Picked off this little one so we wouldn't have too much waste. If this cool weather holds, we should have meat for the rest of the week."

"Not if there's any left when the Alamo Kid catches up," Jakes chuckled. "He can make food disappear faster than a chicken can blink. Saw him win a bet last week that he couldn't finish off a two-pound steak, plus all the fixin's, in ten minutes. When the time was up, he hadn't just polished off the side of beef, but had thrown in a wedge of pie for desert."

"You're pretty fond of that youngster, aren't you?"

"Guess I am. Wouldn't want him to know it, though. He's the best friend I ever had, I can say without question. I wouldn't be seein' today if he hadn't strung along with me to be my eyes, and then have a timely streak of luck with the cards to raise enough dinero to pay for my operation. Between you and the Kid, I really owe a lot. You saved my life and the Kid helped me see again."

"Tell me about him."

Jamison Jakes stopped dressing out the antelope long enough to refill his cup with Platte River and coffee.

"Don't know a lot to tell. At times he can be a struttin' little peacock achin' for a fight, and other times he seems as old and wise as Methuselah. Dependin' on what comes out of his mouth, he can be either my little brother or my father. He's had a hard life for his young age, I do know that. He keeps thinkin' he needs to prove himself to be a man, but he's already proven that to me, many times over."

"I had no idea you felt that strongly about the boy. Tell you what, we can slow our pace some tomorrow and give him a better chance to catch up."

"That's right thoughtful of you, Daniel. He takes a little gettin' used to but I feel in my bones that the two of you will hit it off real good."

The stars were bright and the night icy cold as Jamison Jakes put his head on the saddle he used for a pillow. He pulled his blanket over his chest and pensively sipped his last cup of Platte River coffee. The wrapped carcass of the antelope swung gently from the tree branch, safe from night predators. A few yards away, the snores of Daniel True were the only sounds heard. Then the call of a coyote filled the air and Jamison Jakes thought how unfair it is for any animal, man or beast, to be alone. He considered himself lucky to have not just one, but now two men, he could call friend.

Chapter 12

As promised, Daniel True set a more leisurely pace after the two men broke camp at mid-morning. "We'll just go fast enough to keep the horses from getting too cold," he said. The sky once again looked snow-filled, clouds having arrived in the night, but the wind was calm. The two men had little to say as they rode. There was one question Jamison Jakes wanted to ask, but was waiting for the right moment. In the solitude of a gray noon, he decided the time was right.

"Daniel, what's it like to kill a man?"

"What kind of dumb-assed question is that?" asked the bounty hunter, somewhat annoyed.

"Hey, no offense," Jakes said quickly "I was just wonderin'."

"Didn't you ever kill anyone, boy? You told me you were in the war."

"I don't rightly know if I killed anyone. I fired a lotta rounds into crowds of blue coats enough times, but I don't know if I ever took a man out. Even if I did, I got no idea who it was. No names, nothin' like that. And I maybe killed a renegade Indian who was tryin' to steal some cattle from a drive I was on, but I'm not even sure about that."

"So what you really want to know is what it's like to look a man square in the eye and kill him, is that it?" Daniel True's voice was sharp.

"Yes, but you don't have to say if it's goin' to bother you. I can get along okay without knowin'."

Jakes gave up on the tense discussion and the two men rode on in silence for miles.

"I think about their clothes mostly."

"What's that?" asked a startled Jamison Jakes.

"The men I've killed. Just before I shoot, I think about when they might have buttoned their shirts for the last time, or pulled on their boots, or tied their bandanna. I think about whether they knew that was the last time they'd ever get dressed. A man does something every day of his life, then he does it for the very last time and there he is, waiting to die in that shirt he buttoned and the boots he pulled on.

"And after he's dead, I think that this man was a little boy once. A happy carefree little boy who threw rocks in a pond, and chased cats, and skipped school to go fishing. And I wonder what happened to change that happy little boy into a man so bad that I have to kill him. That's what I think about. Sort of silly, don't you think?"

"No sir, Daniel, not silly at all."

The evening fire had just been lit and an antelope roast placed on a spit above it when a voice called out.

"Hello, the camp!"

"Hello, rider! Come on in!" Jakes responded, recognizing it was the Alamo Kid. "About time you got here."

"Hurried fast as I could. Man, does that hunk a' meat ever look good."

"Be ready pretty soon, Kid, unless you want it mostly raw. It's sure good to see you." Jakes reached toward the Alamo Kid as though he might hug him, then pulled one arm down and extended his hand to vigorously shake the Kid's.

"Mister True," said Jakes, turning toward Daniel True who was busying himself unwrapping his bed roll, "this is my good friend, the Alamo Kid. Kid, this is Daniel True, the man who saved my life in Cheyenne."

"My pleasure, Mister True," said the Alamo Kid cheerfully. "I heard a lotta 'bout you, an' I seen you at the hotel in Denver a few nights back. I didn't know who you was at the time, though."

"And Jamison's told me some about you, Kid. Glad to finally make your acquaintance."

"Kid, do you have 'em?" Jakes asked excitedly.

"You mean them spectacles? Well, I did have 'em. They was all safe an' sound in my saddlebag, but this mornin' that dang horse a' mine stepped on the saddlebag I had layin' on the ground, and smashed them specs to dust!" The Kid winked at Daniel True.

"Goddammit Kid! What a stupid thing to let happen. Why the hell weren't you more careful? Now what am I gonna do?"

Daniel True tried to keep from laughing, but wasn't able.

"What's goin' on?" Jakes demanded to know. "What's so dang funny?"

"The Kid's pulling your leg," True chuckled. "I think he really knows how to yank your rope."

By now the Alamo Kid was also laughing at his own joke.

"Here they be, Preacher, just like they was handed to me by that ol' battle ax in Hopper's office. They even made you up a extra pair like you wanted."

"You little turd!" Jakes smiled as he feigned a swinging blow toward the Kid's head and reached with his other hand to receive the spectacles.

Jakes held the case tightly for a moment, afraid if he

loosened his grip the small package would fly away. Then he slowly opened the top and stared at the wire and glass creation. He held the spectacles by the stems at arm's length and carefully brought them toward his face. He closed his eyes and placed, first one bent wire, and then the other over his ears and pushed the center of the front piece tightly against the bridge of his nose.

"Open your eyes, Jamison," encouraged the Alamo Kid.

"Come on, let's see how they work," Daniel True added.

Jamison Jakes slowly opened one eye and then the other. He blinked a few times then let out a short breath that make a whistling sound as it left his mouth. "My God!" he yelled. "My God, I can see everything like I was right on top of it. It's a sure enough miracle! I couldn't see this good before I was blind!"

Jakes turned in a slow circle, taking in all that could be seen in the glow of the campfire. He allowed his eyes to drink in every shape, every movement of the tree branches swaying in the wind. He followed sparks as they left the campfire and floated off into the darkness and greeted the wisps of smoke that blew toward his face. In the sky, the moon teased his new-found vision as it peered briefly from behind low hanging black clouds, then disappeared.

"Would you look at the grin on his ugly mug?" the Alamo Kid said, breaking the spell.

"Yes, sir," replied Daniel True, "just like a sow getting her back scratched."

While the other two men settled into the routine of setting up camp and were waiting for the meat to finish roasting, Jakes got a full bottle of Platte River from his saddlebag and poured a round of drinks.

"This calls for a celebration," Jakes said eagerly as he handed cups of whiskey to his friends. "A real two-fisted, let's-get-drunk-and-worry-about-it-later celebration."

The Alamo Kid followed his lead and downed the better

part of a cup.

"You hombres best slow down or you're likely to find tomorrow's ride a bit miserable."

"Aw, hell, Daniel, relax a little," responded the Alamo Kid. "There ain't a whole lotta happy things fer a man to drink to. When one comes along, you gotta grab it real quick."

"Well, you fellows do what you need to do, and I'll sure join you in a short one. No disrespect intended if I don't go beyond that."

"None taken," Jakes said lightly. "A man's got his reasons for drinkin' just like another's got his for not. As for me, I wanna have this be a night I remember for a long time."

After another cup of whiskey each, Jamison Jakes and the Alamo Kid sang and laughed and carried around large chunks of meat, eating as they danced around the fire. Daniel True joined in briefly by clapping his hands in tune with "Camp Town Races," but then was content to lie back on his bed roll and watch the party.

The Kid had slowed his drinking considerably, but Jakes kept the pace. He was through his second bottle of whiskey before Jakes' whirling head told him he'd enough fun for one night. He did one last jig and, with a whoop, fell on his blanket. The Alamo Kid squatted next to the fire and sliced off another piece of antelope roast.

Daniel True spoke to the Alamo Kid. "Couldn't help noticing those fancy spurs you're wearing, Kid."

"Ain't they somethin', all right?" replied the Kid. "They's the real things, too. Mexican silver. Ain't no other pair like 'em north a' the Rio Grande."

"Had them long, or did you just come by them lately?"

"Not too long. Won 'em in a poker game."

Daniel True sat up and wrapped his arms around his knees. "You ever been to Thornton, Kid?"

"Nope. Why you askin'?" There was nervousness in the Alamo Kid's voice.

"Kid, do you know how I make my living?"

"Don't rightly know fer sure."

"I work for the law."

"Well, sir, we really need good law in these here parts. We do fer a fact." The Kid's vocal support for law and order was not in keeping with the quizzical look on his face. There was an obvious unease with the direction the conversation was headed.

"The Thornton bank was robbed a while back. Would you know anything about that?"

"Do I look like a bank robber to you, old man?" All friendliness had vanished from the Kid's voice as he picked up the bottle of whiskey from where it had been dropped.

"What's a bank robber supposed to look like?" asked Daniel True as he stood to his feet. "I've seen all types of people end up in the hoosegow for trying to get rich without working for it. Young, old, short, tall, fat, lean. I've even seen a woman go to jail for bank robbery."

"But why you thinkin' I might know somethin' 'bout that Thornton job?" the Alamo Kid persisted.

"It's your spurs, Kid. The hombre who took the Thornton bank wore large Mexican silver spurs. That's all the bank clerk could remember about the robber, but he did remembered those spurs. You said yourself there's not another pair like them north of the Rio Grande. So unless you loaned your spurs to someone, that Thornton thief was you."

Jamison Jakes' sleep was disturbed by the conversation he was hearing, but to his drunken mind it seemed only a dream. He wanted to wake up.

"So what iffen it was me?" asked the Alamo Kid. "I ain't sayin' I done it, but what iffen I *was* the one?"

"I'd need to take you back to stand trial. My job is to bring in men who are wanted by the law."

"But what iffen a man had good reason to need money an' he couldn't get his hands on none an' he went in a place where

they has lots an' he only took what he needed? What then? Is
that guy as bad as the one who steals just fer the hell of it?

"Come on, Mister True, you tryin' to tell me you'd go after
any yahoo who might a' done somethin' that don't amount to a
fart in the wind as soon as you'd go after a killer or rustler?
An' what iffen the man you brung in was innocent, what
then?"

"It's not my place to judge, Kid. I spoke a promise to
myself a lot of years ago that I'd bring in anyone who's wanted
by the law. It's the job of other people to decide if the man I
bring in is guilty."

"You ain't never made no 'ception to that?" asked a
somewhat hopeful Alamo Kid.

"Not one."

Jamison Jakes now realized he wasn't dreaming and tried
to pull himself into a sitting position, but his swirling head
wouldn't leave the saddle on which it was resting.

"Can I tell you a little story?" asked the Kid.

"I always enjoy a good story," replied Daniel True.

"This ain't a good one as it turns out," said the Alamo Kid
sadly. "But it's a honest one, an' I thank you fer lettin' me tell
it. I used to lie a lot. Fact is, my whole life was a lie once.
But I ain't gonna lie now. Though I ain't knowed you more'n
a few hours, I gotta heap a' respect fer you, Mister True, so I
ain't gonna lie. I did rob that bank in Thornton -- but hear me
out. I got my reasons why I done it an' I want you to know
what they is. I never had me a real friend 'til Jamison come
along. I admit he ain't much, but he's my friend."

The Alamo Kid paused for a moment and bit hard on his
lower lip to keep it from trembling. He turned away from
Daniel True's gaze before continuing.

"We needed money so's we could git him that operation to
make him see again. I started out with a few dollars in my
pocket to make a killin' at the poker table, but I went bust real
quick.

"Then I found myself ridin' north, tryin' to figger out what to do, realizin' my friend was layin' there in Denver, countin' on me to bring home the bacon so's he wouldn't be blind no more.

"I ain't never been no good at cards, 'cept the one time when I won them spurs. Anyways, I ended up in Thornton in the early evenin' an' saw this little man gittin' ready to close up the bank an' all a' sudden it 'curred to me they must be a lotta money in there belongin' to folks so rich they wouldn't even miss what I needed to take.

"So as he was lockin' the door, I pushed inside, yanked up my bandanna over my nose, pulled my gun, an' asked that little man fer some money. He was shakin' so bad I told him to lay down on the floor; then I helped myself."

"Yes," interrupted Daniel True, "that's when he got a good look at your spurs."

"Okay, iffen that's what he said. There was a lotta money layin' on that counter, lots more'n we needed fer the operation. So I grabbed me just one sack a' them gold coins an' I took off. Just one sack, mind you. I coulda had it all iffen I'd been a thief. I went to the north a bit more, to throw off the posse an' then circled way back to the east an' then south to get back to Denver."

"Kid, there wasn't a posse formed. You didn't take enough money to earn a posse." Daniel True stated this almost apologetically.

Jamison Jakes somehow managed finally to get to a sitting position and tried to join the conversation, but the messages from his brain to his tongue got garbled and what came out of this mouth sounded like baby-babblings.

Daniel True and the Alamo Kid both looked compassionately in the direction of their prattling friend before the Kid continued.

"Well, I sure wasted me a bunch a' time runnin' from a posse that weren't ever there."

"Kid, you're going to have to let me take you back to Thornton," Daniel True stated emphatically. "You've got to go back and take your medicine. I'm not the only man out here bagging humans for a living. There's a passel of them. If you don't go back and get this cleared up, you'll be looking over your shoulder the rest of your days. That's no way to live, Kid. We'll start for Thornton tomorrow."

"Like hell we will!" yelled the Alamo Kid. "They'll lock me away. I can't stand bein' locked away. My pa throwed me in the tool shed an' kept me there fer days on end. I ain't never gonna be locked up again. If you take me back, it'll be with me hangin' over my saddle. I sure as shittin' won't be alive an' upright."

"That's happened before, Kid. I've taken in a few that way. It'll be a real waste if I have to kill you to get you there."

"That's the only way I'll go. Me and Jamison got plans. We's gonna strike it rich up in the Idaho silver digs. You ain't gonna git in our way, that's fer damn sure."

Jakes, still in a sitting position, shouted in a slurred voice, "Hey, get some sleep and we'll worry about all this in the mornin'."

His vision, though cleared by the spectacles, was still whiskey-hazy.

"Stay out of this!" bellowed Daniel True. "The discussion is between me and the Kid."

"I can't stay out of it! This is all my fault!"

Jakes tried to stand but fell backward into his awkward sitting position.

"Give me your gun, Kid," Daniel True said quietly. "I'm sure when you tell that Thornton jury what you just told me, you'll get off pretty light."

"No way I'm gonna give you my gun," cautioned the Alamo Kid. "Iffen you want it, you gotta take it."

"Don't be stupid, Kid. I'm an experienced gunfighter. You won't have a chance standing up to me."

"Well, iffen I'm ever gonna git started bein' a gunslinger myself, I may's well go up against someone good, an' I got a feelin' you're purty good, Mister True." There was respect in the Alamo Kid's voice.

"I'm damn good, Kid. Now hand over your gun and let's be done with it."

In the seconds that followed, Ellsworth Stipes, now the Alamo Kid, remembered a father who beat him for no good reason and a mother who didn't seem to care. He remembered going to socials with a girl named Janice and the children who laughed at the patches on his pants. He had lived for the day he would be a man, so all that hurt could be assigned to his childhood.

Today he would become a man.

"Okay," he yelled, "here it is!"

As the Alamo Kid reached quickly to fast-draw his gun, Jamison Jakes staggered to his feet screaming "No! Sweet Jesus, no!"

In the instant Daniel True knew the Alamo Kid was drawing down on him and that he would have to defend himself, he looked at the buttons on the Kid's shirt and thought how the Kid had put on that shirt and buckled his silver spurs for the last time. He thought of Tennessee in happier times and the smiling face of the only woman he was ever to love. He wondered if times could be happy again if he just didn't bother to draw. Then instinct took over.

Jamison Jakes heard one shot pierce the cold night air, but saw the flash of two guns, one from each side of the campfire.

"No!" Jakes screamed again.

The Alamo Kid was knocked backward by the force of the bullet to his chest. His body slammed against a tree and he slowly slid to the base of the trunk. Daniel True stood transfixed in the position he had assumed when he had drawn one of his Colts. Then he slumped to his knees and pitched face-forward close to the blazing campfire.

Jakes was still shrieking for his two friends to stop as he lurched toward the stricken figure of Daniel True. He pulled the bleeding man away from the fire and held him in his quivering arms.

"Jamison," whispered Daniel True.

"Yes, Daniel, I'm here.".

"Jamison...tell...Elizabeth..." Before the old warrior could finish his request, his head fell forward onto his chest.

Jakes gently laid the bounty hunter on his back and turned his anxiety to the needs of the Alamo Kid. Jakes crawled across the ground to the tree supporting his young comrade. He reached the Kid and clasped his hand tightly. The Alamo Kid looked like he was just sitting down for an after-dinner smoke; except his eyes didn't blink.

"Preacher."

"Yes, Kid?"

"I coulda took him iffen I'd be sober. You know that, don't you?"

"You did take him, Kid. Mister True is dead."

"You don't say! Well, I got me a good'un first time out, they ain't no denyin' that."

"You did for sure, Kid. He was one of the best."

"Jamison."

"Yes."

"I pissed my pants."

The Alamo Kid stopped breathing. Jakes gently closed the eyes of the man who had just won, and lost, his only gun fight. He wrapped both dead friends painstakingly in their blankets and placed them close to the fire so they would stay warm against the cold nor'easter that was starting to whistle through the ponderosas.

Warm tears streamed down his face as he piled more wood on the fire. He removed his spectacles and placed them in their case, wiping his eyes with the heel of his palm. He found the half- empty bottle of whiskey, fumbled through his saddlebags to locate the remaining two full bottles, stared blankly at one of the labels for a long while, pulled the corks from all three, and poured the brown liquid on the ground.

Jamison Jakes sat against the tree that had supported the dead body of the Alamo Kid.

The plaintive call of a coyote cut through the darkness.

Chapter 13

The nothingness of the night was an adequate companion for Jamison Jakes. He had been there before, but never like this. Empty, lonely, hurting. A gray dawn replaced the glow of the fire telling Jakes his night vigil was over. He had no more tears to cry.

As numbness gave way to reality, he slapped cold water on his face, dried his face with one shirt tail, removed his spectacles from their case and wiped them clean with the other shirt tail. He then had the sad chore of burying his two friends. He searched for grave-digging tools and after a time found a large limb that had been sharpened by a lightening strike and a flat stone that would scrape away the hard topsoil.

It was noon before Jakes was satisfied the holes were deep enough to keep his friends safe from hungry animals. He uncovered the faces of the Alamo Kid and Daniel True; looked at them for some time before covering them again; and secured the blankets tightly around their bodies with lassos.

He moved them slowly, first one then the other, to the side

of their prepared resting places and carefully rolled each into the holes. He used only his hands to cover the bodies, patted the dirt firmly, and placed rocks on top to keep the wild animals at bay. He fashioned two crosses from aspen branches tied together with rawhide strips and pounded them into place at the heads of the two mounds. On the cross marking the grave of Daniel True, Jakes hung two holsters holding wooden handled Colt .45's. On the cross of the Alamo Kid he placed a pair of large Mexican silver spurs.

Jakes wanted to say something, some last words, over his friends. He began by kneeling between the two graves and looking at the ground.

"Well you two were stubborn cusses, I'll give you that. Like two mules, diggin' in your heels and cuttin' no slack. I don't know what to say exactly, except you were my friends, and always will be. I'm sorry I cost both of you your lives. If I'd never been born, or stayed back east where I belonged, you'd be alive today. But I'd be less a man for not knowin' you two. I wish I could've done somethin' to pay you back for all you did for me."

Jamison Jakes looked toward Daniel True. "Mister True...Daniel...thanks for bein' there when I needed you."

Turning to the Alamo Kid, he said "Kid, I love you. I never said those words before, except to my mother. You've shown me what it's like to take life as it comes and deal with it. Thanks for that."

Jakes got to his feet and looked through the branches of a forest of trees to the darkening sky above.

"Hey, Lord! It's me; Jamison Jakes. I'm talkin' at you to let you know a couple of real fine hombres will be stoppin' by your place real soon, if they haven't got there yet. One's an old man with a lot of achin' in his heart for a woman he loved. He's a tall drink of water with long hair and eyes as blue as robins' eggs. The other one just got to be a man not long ago. You'll know him 'cause he just can't stop talkin'. He'll strut a bit when he walks and his spurs make a terrible racket. But he's a good man, God. Please don't judge him by what he did, but by why he did it. I read in your Book once somethin' about you bein' a shepherd and those who join your flock not ever needin' anythin' 'cause there'll always be sweet grass to eat and cool water to drink. And there was somethin' in there about not bein' afraid, even in dark places where wolves and coyotes might be. Well, sir, these two boys don't have to worry about none of that any more. But, Lord, I got worries now that I didn't have when they was with me. I got no idea what to do, or even which direction to take when I leave here. Could you maybe give me a hand and show me what it is I'm supposed to do with my life? I'd be much obliged."

There was a settling calmness that Jakes had seldom felt as he put on his hat and turned away from the two-man cemetery.

What should he do with their belongings? He could set the horses free to fend for themselves; but what about the saddles? Maybe he should take everything back to the relay station and give them to Pappy. They always needed horses of one kind or another at a relay station.

After Jakes had saddled his own horse, he turned his attention to the other two. Picking up the saddlebags that belonged to Daniel True, one of the closing straps came undone and the contents of the bag fell to the ground. There was a tintype photograph and a stack of letters bound together with a piece of twine.

He looked closely at the picture. It was a girl with long golden hair wearing a white dress and holding a cluster of daisies in her hand. She was smiling happily.

"Elizabeth," Jakes said out loud. "That's Elizabeth."

He studied the envelope on top of the stack and pulled it from under the twine. There was no name or address on the envelope, just a date: August 13, 1865. The envelope was sealed. Should he open it, or was this something that should have been buried with Daniel True?

Absence of curiosity was not a part of the make-up of Jamison Jakes. After some moments of running the envelope back and forth between his thumb and index finger, he carefully tore off the end, making sure not to harm the letter. Slowly removing the folded sheet of paper, he knew he was about to enter into Daniel True's private life. As he suspected, the yellowing paper he held in his hand was a letter to Elizabeth.

> *My darling Elizabeth,*
>
> *I hurried home from the fighting as quickly as possible and went directly to your house. No one was there to greet me except your father and he gave me the news, somewhat gleefully, that you had eloped with your beau to Indiana some years before and hadn't returned to Tennessee, even for a visit.*
>
> *I can't tell you the sadness I felt in hearing this. I had so many questions, all of which your father refused to answer. He kept saying "it's all for the best" and let it go at that. Maybe it's all the best for him, but not for me. Maybe it's all the best for you, but not for me.*
>
> *What am I to do, Elizabeth? All my plans were made with you in mind. From the moment you promised to be my wife until yesterday, all I thought of was our future together.*
>
> *Did you care so little for me that you would marry so soon after my departure for the war? What was it that I said, or didn't say, that would make you act with such haste? We sealed our bond so sweetly the night before I left. You were my love, my only love, and you told me I was yours. Was it a lie you said? Was I too old? If so, take pride in the fact that you have made this old man grow older still.*

*That is it, I fear. My age was my enemy
from the start. Even though you said it would
never come between us, I knew it would.*

*But remember how we laughed, Elizabeth?
My Lord, how we laughed.*

Through your love, you made me young.

*I will try to get an address from your family
so I can post this letter. Failing that, I may just
ride up to Indiana and deliver it in person.*

*The weather is very nice today. A bit warm
for me, but you would enjoy it.*

As ever,

Daniel

Jamison Jakes felt his cheeks flush as he finished reading
the letter. He looked at the photograph once more before
putting it away. He was aware of a growing dislike for
Elizabeth.

Replacing the letter in its envelope and returning it to the
top of the pile, he noticed the date on the second: August 13,
1866. He thumbed quickly through the entire stack. Daniel
True had written to Elizabeth each year on the same date.

He decided he would read just one more letter, then head
back to the relay station. Snow was starting to fall as he
opened the second envelope. He removed his spectacles and
put them in their case, as the snow melting on the glass made
reading difficult.

My dearest Elizabeth,

*Well, you know by now that I couldn't get
your Indiana address from anyone; but one of
your childhood friends thought you might be
living in a place named Lawrence. I just didn't
have it in me to try to deliver in person the letter
I wrote last year. So here I am, writing another
that likely will never be read.*

I still think of you each day, and quite often you are in my dreams. Not so much lately as at one time, but nonetheless quite often. I dreamed some nights ago we were at the Ridgeways' for a New Year's party. We had to be so coy so we wouldn't be suspected as being two people in love.

I never told you this, but there was a time, when you were just a girl, that I saw you in a new dress on your way to a gala of some sort. You stopped by the school to show your father how pretty you looked and I couldn't help but stare. That was the day I knew I would love you as a woman. You were thirteen. I promised myself to wait for you. And still I wait, and will forever.

I decided not to continue teaching, so I find myself in Kansas trying to be a cowhand but I'm no good at it. Farmers are beginning to string something called "barbed" wire across open range and it's very hard to cut through at times.

I dislike it when situations get ugly and there is shooting. I had my fill of that in the war.

I end this letter wishing you and yours the very best of everything.

As ever,

Daniel

The temptation to keep reading the letters was great. Jakes wanted to find the key to what had turned a gentle schoolteacher into a bounty hunter. But the day was beginning to close and the snow was falling harder. It was time to move on.

Jakes had one foot in the stirrup when a thought made him hesitate. What was in the Kid's saddlebags? Taking a minute or two to look wouldn't make that much difference. The two empty-saddled horses with their reins tied to the tail of Jakes' bay mare shuffled impatiently.

In the Alamo Kid's bags, Jamison Jakes found a change of clothes, a half-box of pistol cartridges, a plug of chewing tobacco with one bite gone, three picture postcards of naked women, a can of silver polish, and a tin cup and plate. Jakes smiled as he looked at the dog-eared postcards and smiled even more broadly when he reasoned the Kid probably got sick after taking only one chaw off the tobacco plug. He quickly returned the earthly possessions of the Alamo Kid to the saddlebags and chose not to pry anymore into Daniel True's life. Not for the present, anyway.

Snow was falling harder as Jakes looked one last time at the ground embracing his friends then set out at a trot in the direction of the relay station. He knew he wouldn't make it far before darkness stopped him for the night but he needed to get away from where he was.

Riding into the face of the snow, he thought of Daniel True and Elizabeth and the sorrow she had caused. True's last words passed time and again through Jakes' mind, "Tell Elizabeth..." Tell Elizabeth what? That Daniel True is dead? That he never stopped loving her? That he still carried her picture? That he wrote her a letter on the same date each year?

Tell Elizabeth what? Maybe he was to tell her whatever he felt like telling her. One thing was a certainty: Jakes would find Elizabeth, if she still lived. And he would tell her. Damn, how he would tell her.

There was hardly enough light to gather firewood by the time Jakes stopped for the night. He had a blazing fire going before he realized he had nothing to eat. His body craved whiskey. He rolled out his blanket and lay under it close to the fire. To forget the cold and hunger, he brought Daniel True's saddlebags to bed with him. If he was going east to find Elizabeth, he was going to need all the help he could get.

Maybe the bags held a clue.

Much of the contents resembled those found in the Alamo Kid's bags: clothes, shells, eating utensils. Also, rolled together and tied with a string were a number of wanted posters for men who would provide the bounty hunter his livelihood. There was no help as to the exact whereabouts of Elizabeth except the reference to "Lawrence" in True's second letter. Not much, but at least it was a place to start; and Daniel True's first letter had said that Indiana was where Elizabeth had gone with her husband. Jakes would need to see if there was a place called Lawrence, Indiana.

He returned the items to the bags, turned his back to the fire, and attempted to sleep. Jakes suddenly sensed that he was not alone in the camp. Slowly he moved his hand toward the unstrapped pistol lying loose under the blanket. Finding it, he grasped the handle and in one movement threw off the blanket and rolled quickly in the direction of the intruder.

No one. Yet he was sure he was being watched. Why the strong feeling? Thirty-six hours without sleep can make your mind play tricks. Fatigue? Must be fatigue.

He quickly put on his spectacles and pulled on his boots. He went to his saddlebags and instinctively searched for a bottle of whiskey. Finding none, he walked a circle a few yards into the surrounding forest, pistol in hand, until he was sure he was alone. He thought about hitting the trail in the dark but realized that he, and the horses, needed to rest. He couldn't sleep; so after some tossing in his blanket, he retrieved the stack of letters. If he read another letter, maybe sleep would come.

The third letter was dated August 13, 1867.

> *Dear Elizabeth,*
>
> *Why am I so angry with you? It has been seven years since I last saw you and two since I heard the news of your marriage, but there is not a day in my life that you do not invade.*

Can't you just stay away? Is the memory of you stronger than my will to erase you from that memory? How I do want you gone from my mind!

This is the last letter I will ever write you. Even if the letters could be delivered, this would be the last. I must purge you from my thoughts. I must believe that you are not now, never were, or ever will be anything more to me than that little girl I fancied long ago.

You might be pleased to know that I was offered the job of deputy United States marshal for the northeast region of Kansas. I refused. It seemed too confining for my roving spirit.

Your friend,
Daniel True

Drowsiness overcame Jakes at last. He folded the letter, placed it in the envelope and back into the saddlebag, and fell asleep.

Chapter 14

Jamison Jakes' blanket was covered with three inches of powdery snow when he woke from a tormented sleep. From the amount of light, he figured it was about mid-morning. The fire had long since died and Jakes decided not to bother building a new one. He wanted to get back to the relay station before nightfall.

His thoughts dwelled on the events of the past days. He tried to put everything into perspective, to find something positive in all the hurt and confusion he was feeling. He tried, but he couldn't do it. Maybe someday it would all make sense, but this was not the day.

The sky brightened after a few hours, and Jakes was momentarily distracted by the beauty of the countryside as he rode through it. The blanket of soft snow covered everything in a silent whisper. He was aware only of his breathing and the muffled sound of the horses' hooves as they galloped stride after stride through a tapestry of white.

As the afternoon sun cast long shadows toward the east,

Jakes was aware of acrid smoke filling the air. Not a campfire to be sure; too much black smoke for that. A forest fire when everything was wet from the fall rains and now the heavy snowfall wasn't probable. Yet there was the distinct odor of wood burning.

Jamison Jakes spurred his horse into a fast gallop as an uneasy feeling stirred his insides. He remembered that smell from the war years, the stink created by an army in conquest -- or by an army in retreat. It was the pungent stench of a burning building and burning flesh. The only buildings for miles any direction were at the relay station.

Topping the hill, Jakes saw the smoking remains of the large spruce logs that had been the walls of the relay station. He drew blood from the sides of his horse as he demanded more speed from the tired animal and her companions. Arriving in the station yard, Jakes hit the ground running toward what was once the front door of the relay station.

"Pappy!" Jakes yelled. "Pappy, where the hell are you?"

Getting no response, he ran to the back of the smoldering ruins. There he saw a trail of blood in the snow and the marks of a body dragging itself toward the barn, thirty yards to the north. He sprinted toward the barn, slipped in the snow, and slid on his back. He got up, slowed his pace, finally getting to the open barn door. He drew his Colt and moved deliberately through. It was all but dark.

"Pappy!" Jakes shouted again. "You in here?" Still no reply.

He found a lantern hanging on a nail, lit it and began searching the barn. In the second stall, he found Pappy alive but unconscious. Jakes rushed outside, got a hat full of snow, brought it in and rubbed the snow on Pappy's face. In a few minutes, Pappy's eyelids began to flutter.

"Pappy, it's me, Jamison Jakes."

Pappy stared back at the face in front of him. His eyes were glazed and his gaping mouth made Jakes queasy.

"Pappy, can you hear me? Do you know me?"

Jakes put some of the snow on Pappy's lips and Pappy licked it.

"Pappy! Talk to me! It's me, Jamison Jakes! Was it Indians? Did Indians do this to you?"

Pappy pulled open his shirt showing a knife wound to his stomach, a wound much worse than a stab. Pappy's abdominal cavity had been slit open and his intestines were hanging out.

"Pappy! Who did this to you? Tell me!" Jakes was in a rage.

Pappy tried to speak. His lips moved, but words wouldn't come. Then there was nothing but an empty countenance, and Jakes knew Pappy was dead.

He sat for a few minutes, holding the old man's balding head in his hands. He closed Pappy's eyes, reached for a saddle blanket draped over the stall partition and covered Pappy's face. Why did this happen? Who would slaughter this meek old man? Where were the killers now? Was this a part of the same Jakes curse that had delivered the deathblows to Daniel True and the Alamo Kid? Did this kind, simple man die because he, too, had befriended the likes of Jamison Jakes?

"Don't worry, Pappy," Jamison Jakes said firmly. "Whoever sonsabitches did this to you will pay for it, and that's a promise."

It was then Jakes realized there were no horses in the barn. The relay team had been stolen.

"Horse thieves, low-down, filthy, goddamn horse thieves!"

Jakes left the barn to get fresh air. Removing his spectacles to clear the water drops, he noticed a peculiar mound of snow off to the left of the barn. Moving to the pile, he made out the outline of a person underneath. Jakes dropped to his knees and began scooping. Beneath the snow he found the body of the company blacksmith. In his once-powerful right hand he clutched the only weapon he could reach. There was a single bullet hole between his eyes. He had died trying to defend himself, and his friend, with a blacksmith's hammer.

Time and light were wasting while the killers were getting away. Jakes pulled the smithy's body into the barn and placed him alongside Pappy. Then he unsaddled the horses of the Alamo Kid and Daniel True, put them into stalls and fed them a double helping of oats from the feed bin. He quickly poured the contents of Daniel True's saddlebags into his own.

He wrote a note intended for the driver of the next stage coming through:

Stage Driver —
Pappy and the smith was killed by horse thieves
and I'm on the trail of the killers. See to it that they
get buried real good.
Jamison Jakes

The trail left by the killers and the stolen horses was easy to follow, even in the dim light that remained; they were headed north but not following the stage route. Jakes made no camp when night overcame his ability to track. He loosened his horse's saddle and wrapped himself tightly in the three blankets he had taken from the relay station barn. He slept in the dark, waiting for the first light of morning.

No snow fell during the night so Jakes was able to pick up a clear trail in the early dawn. He estimated from the smoldering remains of the relay station that the killers had about a three-hour lead. By mid-morning, the snow began to come down hard and Jakes urged his horse for more speed before the tracks were lost. He still held the anger of the day before and couldn't get rid of the sick feeling in his stomach. Four years of fighting in the war and watching friends die around him had not hardened Jakes to the point of accepting death. But at least death in war had a purpose, or so he still believed. What was the purpose of an old man and a mere boy facing off to die? What was the purpose of human slaughter in trade for some miserable horse flesh?

Jakes was quickly becoming obsessed with a desire to exact something more than just an eye-for-eye revenge when he found the killers. Theirs would be a slow death, he reasoned -- not an ambush. They would know they were going to die and why they were dying. Yes, it would be slow, a little at a time. A shot in the kneecaps, another in the shoulder. Maybe he would make them beg for their lives, groveling on the ground. Then he would truss them up like hogs and slit their throats.

The snow was falling harder, so Jakes pulled his bandanna up over his nose and the brim of his hat down over his spectacles just far enough to keep the snow from hitting them. The tracks of the horses in front of him were filling in less quickly even though the snow was falling heavier. Jakes knew he was gaining on his prey. He was exhilarated. Was this how a bounty hunter feels moving in for the kill? No wonder Daniel True had stayed with it for so long.

Jakes slowed his pace. No need to get eager and lose the benefit of surprise. The killers' path was certain and straight. When darkness fell, he stopped altogether, put one blanket on the ground, wrapped in another, and sat cross-legged with his pistol drawn.

He lapsed into deep thought, trying to remember a time in his life when he wasn't cold, or tired, or hurting. He thought suddenly of when he was ten years old and the daughter of a friend of his mother's came to spend the summer with his family. Her name was Regina and she was also ten. Sometimes she wore his clothes for doing farm chores. They played hop-scotch in the late afternoon when the work was done. Jakes never won. Somehow winning didn't matter. Being with Regina did.

At his mother's urging, Regina tried tutoring Jamison in spelling. His spelling never improved, but he sure enjoyed trying. Her eyes, like tiny stars, seemed to get in the way of his learning.

They swam naked in Jessamine Creek before they knew it was wrong. They were ten years old and didn't even giggle when they stripped. Didn't know they were supposed to. One day they were caught by Joshua Jakes, who found them swimming, and they got spanked hard. They were told in loud, no uncertain, terms that it was something called a 'sin' to swim naked with each other.

The summer ended and Regina was gone as quickly as she had come. Just before Christmas of that year, the Jakes family got word that Regina had died of pneumonia. Jamison was in sorrow for days. To him, pneumonia was contracted by playing hop-scotch, complicated by spelling lessons and a girl wearing boy's pants, and was the fatal result of the sin of swimming naked in Jessamine Creek, in the summer when you are ten.

Jamison Jakes stared at the hard-falling snow and shook his head sadly. Even when he tried to think of something full of life, his thoughts turned to death. His eyelids were heavy; he fought the goading of his body for sleep. His plan was to wait an hour or so then walk, leading his horse through the trees in the darkness, until he found the killers' camp.

He lost the fight.

Jakes shook himself awake after some hours and scrambled to his feet like he'd been stung by a hornet. In the darkness he was disoriented and his sudden movements spooked his horse. The mare would have bolted if she hadn't been hobbled. In her panic, she reared on her hind legs and fell sideways into the deep snow. She laid there until Jakes could reach her and give quiet reassurances that all was well.

Then he saw it. Not more than two hundred yards ahead was the orange glow of a dying camp fire. The killers! Right in front of him! If he hadn't stopped when he did he would have overtaken the murdering thieves in a darkness that would have been his foe rather than his ally.

Had they heard the commotion his horse made when she fell? Maybe not. The wind was blowing hard through the trees and Jakes was downwind of his prey. There was no stirring in the camp site.

"Thank you, Lord," he whispered.

Jakes took his rifle from its scabbard and moved slowly and quietly toward the orange glow. Everything was in his favor now: a point of light guiding him through the snow-filled blackness; the element of surprise in the middle of the night; the fatigue of his unsuspecting quarry.

Thirty yards from the clearing, Jakes fell to his stomach and moved forward like a giant reptile, cradling his rifle in the hollow of the elbows that were supporting his weight. He moved inches at a time, waiting after each short advance to make sure he hadn't been detected. In the dying light of the fire, just to the right of him, he could make out the outlines of horses standing in a row. Noiselessly he got to his feet and moved, one slow step after another, toward the horses. Reaching them, he counted four draft horses and one saddle horse.

One man! Only one man! The killer was by himself!

Holding his breath, Jakes cut the ropes that tethered each horse. He knew the drafts would find their way back to the relay station and that the saddle horse would follow. At least the stage company would be one horse ahead. Small compensation for a relay station master and a blacksmith, but it was something.

Jakes studied the motionless form sleeping on his back with his head propped against a saddle. As Jakes inched forward, he could distinguish the profile of the man under the blankets. He was big – well over six feet – and his ample stomach and chest pushed hard against the blankets with each snorted intake of air.

Jakes was terrified but his anger overrode his fear. At last he would be face to face with the man who had brutally slaughtered two good men. Jakes held his cocked Winchester at the ready as he approached the snow-covered heaving mass. In the last blush of firelight, Jakes could see the killer's gun in his gloved hand, outside the blanket. Jakes' body began to shake as he stood over the man. Then, with all the force he could muster in his chilled body, he stomped hard with the heel of his boot on the hand holding the gun and ground it into the snow.

"What the hell!" wailed the big man.

His deep voice bellowed through the mountains and echoed across the cold darkness. Jakes heard the five startled horses running away to the south. The killer's eyes had opened wide and he was looking straight up the barrel of Jakes' rifle. Jakes looked down at the astonished man and felt the pressure building in his trigger finger. This was the moment for which he had waited.

But his finger would not respond to the mandate of his malice. As much as he wanted to send a skull-shattering bullet through the brain of the wide-eyed bastard on the ground in front of him, he couldn't do it.

"On your stomach!" Jakes yelled while picking up the killer's pistol. "Roll over on your stomach!"

"Don't kill me! Please don't kill me!" The coward was pleading, just like Jakes had wanted.

"I got money, if it's money you're after. I'll give you all my money. And horses. I got horses. I got money and horses and I'll gladly give 'em to you if you just don't shoot me."

"Shut your goddamn mouth!" Jakes anger was partly directed at himself for not being able to pull the trigger.

As the enormous mass struggled to stand, Jakes brought the butt of his Winchester down hard on the back of the killer's head. The man groaned and pitched forward into the snow. Jakes quickly reached for the lasso on the saddle lying on the ground and tied the hulk's hands tightly behind his back, then looped the rope around the murderer's feet and pulled hard to hog-tie him. Satisfied the knot was secure, Jakes lashed his captive to a tree, wrapped a blanket around him, stoked the dying fire, and added wood. Within minutes the area was brightly lit for yards in every direction.

Jakes searched the man's belongings for weapons. He found two more pistols, a sawed-off shotgun, and a large buffalo skinning-knife. This was the knife, Jakes concluded, that had been used to slit Pappy open. At the bottom of a worn saddlebag, wrapped in a piece of burlap, was a wad of money. In the other pocket of the bag, Jakes found a full bottle of whiskey. Out of habit, he took the cork from the bottle and moved the bottle toward his mouth. He ran his dry tongue over his chapped lips and inhaled the aroma of the brown liquid. Just a few swallows of this fire-filled treasure, his spent mind told him, and he would gain the courage to use the shotgun to blow the head off this slimly assassin. He put the cork back in the bottle and tossed the bottle on the ground.

Jakes was the flag on the rope in a tug-of-war. Walking through the woods to get his horse and other belongings, Jakes disposed of the guns, tossing them into snow drifts. By the spring thaw, the guns would be rusted and useless if they were ever found. He would keep the skinning knife. Returning to the place where he had dropped the bottle, Jakes took a deep breath and then, against the side of a large ponderosa, smashed to pieces the full bottle of whiskey.

It was only after returning to the horse thief's camp and wrapping himself in a blanket, that Jakes took time to look at the face of his trussed-up captive. Something about the bastard seemed familiar. Had he seen this animal somewhere before?

Then Jakes remembered the roll of wanted posters Daniel True had been carrying. He got them from his saddlebag and looked at each one carefully. Near the bottom of the stack he found the likeness of the man lying in front of him. He was Emory Gordon, better known as the Widowmaker.

Chapter 15

What terrible irony, Jamison Jakes thought as he searched for more firewood. Daniel True had guessed right. The Widowmaker was headed to Cheyenne, but on a different trail. Maybe the bloody activity at the relay station changed the killer's plans and made him head off in another direction, so the bounty hunter might not have found him anyway. That question would never be answered for Daniel True.

Jakes couldn't allow himself to sleep. The Widowmaker was tied tightly enough and remained unconscious, but Jakes was still concerned about what might happen if Jakes fell asleep and was caught off guard. He busied himself melting snow in his coffee pot and pouring the hot water into the almost-empty canteens.

Finishing that task, he sat on a blanket near the fire and read the Emory Gordon wanted poster. *Murder. Rape. Bank Robbery. Rustling.* How could one man go so sour? Jakes figured the five-thousand dollar reward offered for bringing in this menace dead or alive would be money well spent by the Cheyenne Merchants for Decent Living Committee, the group offering the reward.

It was only then Jakes realized he was in line for the reward. Five thousand dollars! That was more money than he had ever seen together at one time, let alone held in his hands. Five thousand dollars! All he had to do was deliver this bag of skunk shit to Cheyenne and the money was his.

Maybe his luck was changing.

As Jakes returned the poster to the roll and placed them in the saddlebag, he saw again the stack of Daniel True's letters. Reading a letter would occupy his mind in the middle of a cold, lonely night.

He searched for the next letter and opened the envelope dated August 13, 1868.

> *My dearest Elizabeth,*
>
> *It was not possible for me to follow through with my promise to never write you again. That was something that I needed to say for myself, to strike out at you, to show my anger.*
>
> *But, truth be known, I have been eagerly waiting for this day, this anniversary, so I could apologize for that anger. Forgive me for blaming you for my own mistakes.*
>
> *Elizabeth, my darling Elizabeth, you are always in my thoughts. And my dreams. I sometimes choose to imagine that you died when I was away fighting. I take comfort in this thought from time to time, that you did not leave me to love another, but that you died while waiting for my return. Oh, it was not a painful death, to be sure. You simply fell asleep one night thinking of your love for me, and just didn't awaken in the morning. This way I can pretend that you are in heaven rather than with*

someone other than me.

Does that sound like the reasoning of a jealous man, to wish you dead rather than alive with someone else? Then so be it. I am a jealous man. I prefer to think you are mine only. Then, now, and forever.

I can take no comfort in the fact that I was your first love unless I can convince my somewhat deranged mind that I am also your only love.

Yet, in truth, I know that you are a married woman and undoubtedly have a number of children at this time in your life. By my counting you are twenty-four years old now. My conjecture is that you have three offspring, two boys and a girl. I hope they fancy you in looks. If so, they are most fortunate.

Elizabeth, do you remember the day we went riding by the river? The sun was warm and we could hear the crickets on the river bank and you made up a song about them? I recall the words but not the tune. Have you taught your children the cricket song?

The grunting sounds of the Widowmaker regaining consciousness interrupted Jakes' reading. Jakes stood and offered the big man a drink of water from the canteen, wrapped his bandanna around a ball of snow, squeezed the snow into a small ice pack, and placed the cold compress on Gordon's swollen head. Then he returned to the letter.

I wonder if you have ever told your husband about us and, if so, what he thinks. Does he get along well with your father? I hope so, for your husband's sake. Your father, for all his good intentions, can be a harsh man. Even cruel if he feels the occasion calls for it.

*I close now with the promise that I will
continue to write, for my sanity hangs in the
balance.*
With loving thoughts,
Daniel

Emory Gordon was now fully awake and lay on his side looking menacingly at Jamison Jakes throwing more wood on the fire.

"When we gonna eat?" the Widowmaker snarled. "Or are you plannin' to starve me to death?"

"If you got nothin' to eat, and I know you don't because I've been through your things, then there's nothin' to eat," Jakes replied. "You can fill up on snow for all I care. There's plenty of that."

"Who the hell are you anyway?" asked Gordon. "And why'd you come chargin' in here lookin' to kill me? I ain't never laid eyes on you."

"That's for sure, you bastard. You don't know me from Satan. Let's just say we had mutual friends. One was ready to track you to kingdom come and haul your fat ass to jail. The other was the man you slit open back at the relay station." Jakes felt his anger growing.

"That old man had lived long enough and he was beggin' to get killed," growled Gordon. "Never saw a man so dumb as to look a pig-sticker straight on and then spit in the face of the hombre holdin' it. A jackass that dumb shouldn't be allowed to live."

Jakes thought for a minute about getting out the skinning knife. Maybe the Widowmaker would sing a different tune if he saw the big blade coming close to his own fat belly. Jakes wondered if he could ever bring himself to look a man in the eye and cut out his guts without remorse. He hoped he'd never find out.

Before continuing the hard trip north to Cheyenne, Jakes untied the legs of the Widowmaker but kept his hands bound behind his back. Then he put another lasso around the waist of Emory Gordon and tied the loose end to the bay mare's saddle pommel.

Jakes mounted and started off at a walk, pulling his reluctant prisoner after him.

"Hey, wait a minute for God's sake!" Gordon yelled. "Where's my horse? You ain't gonna make me walk!"

"Your horse is headed back to the relay station with those you stole. And you sure as hell are gonna walk, or get dragged, all the way to Cheyenne. Makes no difference to me."

"Cheyenne's a good two days from here. I can't walk that far! It'll kill me!"

"Don't matter to me if you die," responded a hardened Jamison Jakes. "I get five thousand dollars whether you walk in or get dragged in. And it don't matter none if you're dragged in alive or dead. It's all the same to me, and it's all the same to the good folk in Cheyenne. If you're dead, it'll save them the cost of a trial."

"So that's the way it's gonna be, eh?" asked the Widowmaker slowly. "You want me dead, but you ain't man enough to kill me. I know the likes of you. Tough man with the mouth but no balls to back up the words. I've killed a few of you puppies. And before we get anywheres near Cheyenne, I'll have done killed me another." The Widowmaker chuckled at the thought.

"You sounded pretty gelded yourself a few hours back when I had the drop on you and you were beggin' for your life. Don't suppose it felt too good, lookin' up the business end of a Winchester. I could've sent you straight to hell then, except I remembered the words of a man I truly respect who told me it was one job to take in a wanted man, but another job for people to decide his guilt. If I was an animal like you, I would've splattered your pug-ugly face and been done with it. But the killin's got to stop somewhere. You don't keep killin' because killin's been done. It's got to stop; otherwise there'll be nobody left in the world."

With that, Jamison Jakes urged his horse forward at a faster pace, pulling the bound Widowmaker behind at a trot.

The serenity of the autumn noontime was broken by the obscenities bellowing from Emory Gordon's mouth as he walked, and stumbled, and then ran to keep up with Jakes' horse.

Jakes ignored the man by thinking of Maryalice Wheeler. What would she be doing now, at this time of day? Probably getting dressed to go to work in the café and worrying if her hair was looking all right or if her petticoat was showing. Would she be thinking of him just now, as he was thinking of her? If so, what were her thoughts? Not good, he figured, considering the circumstances under which he had left. What if he had stayed? Would things be different? For sure, the Alamo Kid and Daniel True would still be alive. Pappy and the blacksmith would be dead, of course, because Jakes had nothing to do with their fate. The Widowmaker would have been at the relay station regardless of where Jakes was at the time the killer arrived. But the Widowmaker might then still be free, for Daniel True would have thought he was still ahead of them instead of behind. Hard to know how that might have turned out.

What made Jakes run from Denver? Maryalice was nice and very pretty. She made no demands on him. And yet he ran. In hindsight, not one of his better decisions, he thought. But, by his own admission, Jamison Jakes was a runner. However, he admired those who could stay in one place and from time to time he would be envious of the life of a merchant or farmer or rancher who was born and bred in one locale then married and had children and grandchildren who stayed close to home and finally was buried, generation beside generation, in the family graveyard.

If there was ever a person in Jamison Jakes' life to make him stop running, he knew for a fact that person was Maryalice Wheeler.

Jakes' daydream was abruptly interrupted as he felt his horse slip on the snowy trail and begin to fall to one side. Jakes was able to leap from the horse's back before he was caught and pinned to the ground by the weight of the animal. He quickly drew his Colt as he struggled to find his footing.

Emory Gordon was a few feet away from his surprised captor, and approached him quickly. One heavy boot toe caught Jamison Jakes in the groin and for a moment the world went black as he sank to his knees. As Jakes fought to regain his feet, he was aware that Emory Gordon was attempting to mount the horse. Jakes rushed toward the man and pulled him hard to the ground. The excited horse bolted and ran for thirty yards before she stopped, having dragged a cursing Emory Gordon through snow drifts.

When Jakes caught up with the horse, he all but ignored the condition of the Widowmaker, lying face down in the snow. When Jakes turned him over, Emory Gordon lashed out with his feet and filled the air with swearing. Jakes kicked him hard in the ribs to shut him up.

Dusk was turning to dark by the time the skittish horse had settled enough to continue, so Jakes decided instead to make camp. He led his horse, which in turn, pulled the Widowmaker, until he found a clearing large enough for a campsite. Wet snow was falling fast and dry wood was hard to come by but Jakes was able to get enough together to last for a few hours, at least until the horse had had a chance to rest and Jakes' bruised groin could heal some.

Emory Gordon was exceptionally quiet, tied in a sitting position to a tree next to the camp fire. His face was still purple from being dragged through the snow. The Widowmaker, at last, seemed resigned to his fate. Jakes boiled water from melted snow as soon as the fire was hot enough. He held a cup to the Widowmaker's lips and he accepted the water without comment. Jakes pretended his hot water was steaming black coffee served to him by a dark-haired blind girl in far away Denver. The pretending helped some, but not a lot.

In the restless hours that followed, Jakes gave in to his desire for sleep, but never totally succumbed. He nodded off for a few minutes at a time, allowing his mind to associate freely with whatever came strolling through it. He saw a river bank and felt the warm sun and listened to crickets and wondered what song they sang to people in love. He imagined a tall scholar standing next to a fair-haired young woman as she busied herself setting out a picnic lunch.

Warmth...food...two people in love.

Was there more to life than this? There need not be, at least for Jamison Jakes. She was a lovely woman, this Elizabeth, this breaker of promises and hearts, this object of worship. Come, lay down, Elizabeth, here in the warm sun and listen as the crickets sing love songs. Do they sing for us?

Morning finally arrived and Jakes broke camp after letting Emory Gordon drink two cups of hot water. By his best guess they could make Cheyenne by noon the next day if the Widowmaker could keep the pace. Considering the volume of snoring coming from Gordon's sleeping body, Jakes concluded he was plenty rested. But Jakes' body cried out for solid sleep. His stomach rumbled and he couldn't remember his last meal. He had been dumb to cut all the horses loose, he chastised himself. Just one of them would have provided more than enough meat for the trip.

Jakes was taking no chances of repeating the problem of the day before. Rather than place the leading lasso around the Widowmaker's waist, Jakes looped it around Gordon's neck and pulled it secure, allowing just enough slack for him to breathe without difficulty. Jakes then took the precaution of tying himself into his saddle before they started out. This way, if he fell asleep on the trail, he at least wouldn't lose his mount.

The journey had only started when Jamison Jakes' mind began to play its trick once again.

"Private Jakes!"

"Yes, Sergeant."

"I'm looking for a volunteer."

"For what, Sergeant?"

"That farm house down there seems to be empty, but we can't be sure. May be full of Bluebellies. I need you to sneak down there and find out which is true."

"By myself, Sergeant?"

"Of course by yourself! Iffen they's nobody there, one man's all we need to get the message. On the other hand, iffen they's Bluebellies there, then no need in more'n one man gittin' killed. Don't you agree?"

"I guess that makes sense, Sergeant."

"Course it does. Now git on down there. Check out everythin'. 'Specially the barn. Don't forget the barn."

As his horse struggled once again with her footing on the slushy trail toward Cheyenne, Jamison Jakes' weary mind had taken him to a hot day in the autumn of his first year in the Army of the Confederacy, and now he was advancing alone on a farm house just across the Kentucky border in Tennessee. A farm house that could be filled with Union soldiers.

"You go get 'em, Jakes," his sergeant called in a loud whisper as the sixteen-year-old fighting man moved stealthily toward the foreboding house. *"Let us know iffen you need help!"*

Jamison Jakes smiled at the memory as the snow hit his spectacles, making it difficult to see the trail ahead. He looked back at the Widowmaker to let Gordon know he hadn't been forgotten. Then, as quickly as he had left it, Jakes was back in Tennessee.

On his stomach now, he inched toward the farm house that could well be a Union outpost. Sweat steamed from every pore of the child-warrior as he got within spitting distance of the house. He crawled, ever so quietly, to a large front window. Slowly he looked inside. Nothing. He crawled along the side of the house to another window and, while holding his breath, quickly looked through the glass. Nobody. He slithered on his stomach to the back of the house. Another window, another chance to see the enemy. No one there! The house was empty!

"Can we stop for a rest? You're walkin' my ass off!" The yelling of Emory Gordon jerked Jamison Jakes out of a hot Tennessee afternoon and back to the Colorado snow.

"Not now!"

"I gotta stop for a while. My legs feel like fire's pourin' through 'em."

"We'll stop when I say we stop!"

Don't forget the barn, Jakes told himself. The sergeant specifically had ordered him to check the barn. Why would there be soldiers in the barn if there were none in the house? But the sergeant said to check the barn, so the barn would be checked.

As quietly as possible Jakes moved toward the open barn door. He removed the bayonet from his waist belt and snapped it into position at the end of his rifle. He took three deep breaths and rushed inside the barn.

Empty! All right! All right! Empty. No enemy. Private Jamison Jakes had done his job. He had crawled and sweated into the face of the enemy and found them gone. Hot damn! He did his job and was alive to tell about it!

"For God's sake, let me rest!" Emory Gordon was staggering with each step he took in the heavy snow.

"Okay, we'll stop for ten minutes; then we've got to go at least another five miles."

"Why don't you just shoot me and put me out of my misery? If we keep this pace, I'm a goner anyway."

In ten minutes the two were back on the trail and Jakes had returned to Tennessee.

"Hey, Johnny Reb! Up here!" Private Jakes stiffened with

fright. It was a woman's voice. "Here I am, come on up. I been waitin' for you. What took so long? I was about to get started without you."

Although fearful of what he might find, Jamison Jakes carefully followed the sound of the voice coming from the barn loft. He found the ladder to the upper level and climbed up, one apprehensive step at a time. Cautiously peering into the loft, he saw a woman, a naked woman, lying in the hay fondling her breasts.

"Hi, soldier, come on up and get comfortable."

Jakes couldn't speak. He could only watch, not believing what he was seeing.

"Come to Momma, little boy. I ain't gonna hurt you. Momma's got a present for you from your friends. It's all paid for, too."

Fifteen minutes later, Jamison Jakes exited the barn to the cheering and whistling of his comrades. The broad grin on his face was all the thanks his buddies needed.

"Damn you! I can't keep this up! What's your big hurry anyway? Cheyenne ain't goin' nowhere." The Widowmaker continued to complain while Jakes scanned his memory to find more warmth from the past.

In this state, Jakes was oblivious to the terrain, simply giving his horse rein and allowing her to pick the trail.

When it happened, it happened so fast that Jakes could do nothing to stop it. First, he felt his horse slipping once more to the ground, falling on her side and pinning Jakes' leg underneath. The mare's belly slid hard into the trunk of a large ponderosa and she wheezed loudly as the wind was knocked from her lungs. Then Jakes heard the scream of Emory Gordon and looked helplessly as the Widowmaker plunged over the precipice a few yards from the side of the trail. The lasso pulled taut when the full weight of the big man strained against the knot holding the rope to the pommel.

Jakes untied himself from the saddle and dug his pinned

leg from under the horse, which was still struggling to catch her breath. He pulled hard on the rope, trying to bring Gordon up from the rim of the ravine, but the Widowmaker was too large a load.

Cut him loose, Jakes told himself. Cut him loose or he'll be hanged. Jakes reached for the skinning knife in his saddlebag and looked down at the man swinging at the end of the lasso. The huge man's legs twitched a few times, and then there was no movement. In the shadows of the falling snow, Jakes couldn't see the bottom of the ravine.

Jakes tried once more to pull the big man to the top, and urged his horse to stand so she could help pull, but the ground was too slick and the weight too much. Knowing that Emory Gordon, the Widowmaker, was dead, Jakes cut the rope and listened as the body fell far below to its final resting place.

"It's going to be a hard winter," Jakes said to his horse as she finally got to her feet. "Maybe he'll keep a coyote or two alive."

Chapter 16

The ride into Cheyenne took most of the following day. Jamison Jakes spent the better part of an hour after the sun rose looking for a way down to retrieve the Widowmaker's body from the snowy ravine, but it wasn't possible.

Jakes was tightly wound in the arms of fatigue when he finally got to the livery stable on the edge of town. There was no one around, but the door was unlatched so he went inside and fed his horse. Even though his own hunger was ravenous, Jakes couldn't fight the ache to burrow into a mound of hay; in no time he was sleeping.

Seconds later, it seemed, the night was over and the sun was streaming through the barn window onto Jakes' face. He got up, relieved himself in the corner, went outside, broke through the layer of ice in a watering trough, and washed his face.

Cheyenne felt like an old friend as he looked down the long street that led to the town center. The rumble of his empty stomach broke the silence, and he walked quickly to the café at the Hobson House, eager to break his three-day fast.

"Well, lookee who's here!" shouted the cook as Jakes strode through the door. "As I live and breathe, it's Mister Jakes! How the hell are you? You're lookin' mighty fine; yes sir, mighty fine!"

"I'm a heap better than when I left, Cookie," Jakes said with a wide grin. He liked the fact he was recognized. "Got my eyes back with the help of that Denver doc and these spectacles."

"Well, sir, folks 'round here'll be mighty pleased to hear that. Cheyenne people don't forget their heroes none too quick."

"That's good, Cookie. That's real good."

He wanted to say more, wanted to bend the little fat man's ear about how desperately he needed a friend and how he had just lost the companionship of both Daniel True and the Alamo Kid and how the loneliness was gnawing at his gut. But he kept quiet, put the two saddlebags he was carrying under the table, sank deeply into a chair, and ordered a big breakfast.

This is where it all began, Jakes reminisced while waiting for his food. Right over there Daniel True sat and gave him that first knowing look. There on the wall hung the slateboard with the menu the Alamo Kid couldn't read. Had it only been such a short while? He had lived a lifetime since he last sat in this room. What would happen next? He had a five-thousand dollar reward coming for killing the Widowmaker. Five thousand dollars! That's more money than he could make in three years working as a cowhand. A large steak, four eggs, a half-dozen biscuits and a pot of coffee later, he registered for a room and ordered a bath.

The wooden tub was quickly delivered to the room, but Jakes was told it would be an hour before the hot water would be ready. He pulled off his boots for the first time since the night his friends had died, stretched out on the bed, removed his spectacles, and stared at a fuzzy ceiling. He tried to block out all thought, to close his eyes and see nothing but blackness, to lose himself in dark warmth where he might find some blessed rest.

Tomorrow he would think again. Tomorrow he would be warm again. The dirt and the fatigue would be washed away by tomorrow. Tomorrow he would pick up the pieces of his broken life and start again. Tomorrow...tomorrow...

Jamison Jakes' listless body ached for a swallow of whiskey. Those days and nights on the trail had been so hectic that he hadn't had time to even think about a drink, although his body wouldn't let him forget how much he had been missing whiskey. Just one drink. He'd earned at least that much after all he had been through. He'd lost his two best friends, saw a man who'd been slaughtered, captured a devil, and withstood cold days and long nights without sleep. He wanted a drink! He deserved a drink! By damn, he was going to go downstairs and get a drink!

"No!" Jamison Jakes heard his own voice shout.

He gripped the brass head rails. Beads of sweat covered his brow and he felt his body shaking. The pain in his stomach drew his knees to his chest.

"Oh, God! Dear God! What's happening? What's wrong with me?"

In the swirling darkness of his struggle not to think, and over a distance that couldn't be measured, Jakes began to hear a faint jingle. In his writhing pain, he tossed from side to side as the sound grew louder. There were no footsteps, just the rhythmic cadence of a jingling sound.

Shades of black flashed to grays and back again. Stomach cramps became unbearable and the groans of a man thought to be dying filled the room.

Spurs! The jingle of spurs -- large Mexican spurs!

The blackness abated. The pain subsided. Stomach muscles relaxed. Bloodshot eyes, filled with tears from gut-wrenching torment, slowly opened.

An ethereal form stood at the foot of the bed.

"Well, Preacher, I see you be flat on your back again."

"Kid? Kid is that you?"

"Well, iffen it ain't, I'm wearin' someone else's longjohns."

"But, Kid, you're...you're..."

"Dead?"

"Yeah, dead."

"Well, sir, I reckon that's what they call it, but you can't prove it by me. I don't feel dead. Matter a' fact, I don't feel nothin' a' tall. Don't feel no pain. The sun ain't hot an' the night ain't cold. The wind seems to blow right through me. I go places without gittin' on a horse, an' I never git tired. Never have to sleep or eat neither. But the whole time I feel like I just woke up from a good night's rest with my tummy full a' home cookin'."

"Kid, I'm just dreamin' this. It's not real. I been on the trail so long without sleep that I dozed off and didn't even know it."

"Preacher, iffen you need to think you're sleepin' fer us to be jawin' this a' way, then go right on sleepin'. As fer me, I'm just enjoyin' the visit."

"Okay, Kid, I won't fight it. But I got to admit, I'm a little spooked."

"Nothin' to be spooked 'bout, Jamison. It's just me. Ain't nothin' changed, 'cept my body feels light as a goose feather."

"How did you find me?"

"Don't rightly know. Seems like I was with a bunch a folks and someone was talkin' 'bout a visit he'd just made an' I started thinkin' I sure would like to have just one more visit with ol' Jamison Jakes -- an' then here I was in your room."

"What did you want to talk about, Kid?"

"Oh, nothin' special. Just wanted to make sure you was all right an' didn't need no more lookin' after. An' to say thanks fer all you done fer me an' to let you know how bad I feel 'bout lettin' you down. That more'n anythin', I reckon. Don't think I coulda been at peace with myself iffen I didn't let you know I be sorry. I be real sorry, Jamison."

"Hey, Kid, I'm sorry, too. Sorry things ended up the way they did. God sent you to me, Kid. I'll never forget you or your kindness."

"Then, can we call it even? Can we both be happy that we was friends an' have no hard feelin's 'bout each other?"

"We were the best of friends, Kid. There'll never be another like you."

"Then I'll be on my way so's you can get that bath you're needin'."

"Don't go Kid! I don't want you to go."

"Sorry, Preacher. I can't 'splain it, but I know I'm leavin' now an' there ain't nothin' I can do 'bout it."

"Will I see you again, Kid? Will you be able to come back?"

"Don't know how that works. Guess I gotta come this time 'cause I really needed to talk with you. Just don't know how it works. So long, Preacher."

Jamison Jakes listened as the sound of jingling spurs became faint, and finally silent.

"So long, Kid," Jakes mumbled. "So long."

Jamison Jakes slept the entire day and most of the night, and when he finally woke the pain was mostly gone from his body. He wasn't sure if all he remembered about the visit from the Alamo Kid was real or a dream.

The bathtub had been filled with water and, although it had gotten cold, he climbed into the tub and scrubbed himself. Then he quickly dressed and went directly to the sheriff's office to file his reward claim.

"Howdy, Sheriff. Name's Jakes. Jamison Jakes."

"And I'm Rex Malcolm. Pleased to meet you. I was out

on a chase the last time you was in town, but I got an earful about you when I got back. What's your pleasure?"

"I'm here to put in a claim for the reward on Emory Gordon. Some folks call him the Widowmaker."

"You got the Widowmaker? Man, if that's so, you really hit the jackpot! Where you got him stashed?"

"Well, sir, he's at the bottom of a ravine about twenty miles south of here."

"You mean, you ain't got him with you?"

"Nope, but he's the Widowmaker all right. No question about that. I got a wanted poster with his picture on it and was with him for the better part of two days. We talked about some of the things he'd done and I saw first-hand some of the things he'd done right after he'd done them. He's the Widowmaker all right."

"That may well be, Mister Jakes. But you see, before I can file a claim for you, I got to have proof positive that he's who you say he is. For sure, the poster says dead or alive but I got to have more'n just your word for it."

"You callin' me a liar?" Jakes asked, feeling the start of irritation.

"No, I ain't callin' you a liar. It's just that there's rules to follow. If you bring a wanted man in, you get the reward. If you don't, you don't get nothin'. Them's the rules of the bounty-huntin' game. You must be new at this."

"I'm not a bounty hunter," Jamison Jakes responded through tightening lips. "I'm just a man who saw what that animal did and was bringin' him in for it. He could've killed me but he didn't have the chance. I could've killed him after I tracked him down, but I didn't because someone taught me it was the job of others to do that, after a fair trial. Well, he got himself killed anyway. Now you're tellin' me that because I can't produce that ugly bucket of horse shit, I don't get the reward?"

"Them's the rules. I truly am sorry. I believe you had him.

I believe he's dead. The world will rest a bit easier tonight with him gone from it. But all I can give you is my thanks."

Jamison Jakes knew that no amount of telling the entire story of how Gordon died would change the sheriff's mind. After all, Jakes reasoned, it wasn't for money that he'd gone after the Widowmaker in the first place. In fact, he didn't even know who Emory Gordon was until after he'd caught him.

But, Lord, how he could have used that reward money...

The day was bitter cold when Jakes got back to his hotel. He threw some wood into the potbelly stove that heated the room, rubbed his hands together in front of the open stove door, then closed it with his foot and walked to the window. Snow was falling in tight swirls and heavy dark clouds hung over the high plains. Alone in this vast frontier land, his life half-spent, he reflected on what he considered to be the nothingness of his existence.

More from curiosity than by design, Jakes hauled out the two saddlebags he had hidden under the bed and dumped the contents of one on the quilt. The last earthly possessions of Emory Gordon, the Widowmaker, tumbled out.

The burlap package! The money! During the frenzy of the last days, Jakes had completely forgotten about the Widowmaker's money. He unwrapped the greenbacks and spread them on the bed. One-hundred dollar bills, all of them. Nothing but one-hundred dollar bills.

Jakes counted out the bills and put them in stacks of ten. When he finished there were six stacks with ten bills each and one stack with four.

"Sixty-four hundred dollars," Jakes said with a whistle. "Sixty-four hundred dollars! That's a heap more than the reward money. Maybe times won't be so bad after all."

Chapter 17

Jamison Jakes was in a quandary. His brain was trying its best to adjust to the lack of whiskey and his body was still in a world of hurt from the long days and nights on the trail. He wasn't at all sure of his next move. He'd promised himself that he would carry out Daniel True's dying request to "tell Elizabeth" whatever he could concoct that the old man wanted her to know. But Cheyenne was a long way from Lawrence, Indiana. Even if he went there, he had no idea how to find her.

On top of that, he was now a rich man. The fleeting notion that he should turn in the sixty-four hundred dollars quickly gave way to the rationalization that no one could ever determine from where that particular money was stolen. The rightful owner would never get it back anyway.

If the law wouldn't allow Jakes to get what he'd earned by capturing Emory Gordon, then to hell with the law.

With this much money he could buy a spread and a few head of breed stock and settle down as a rancher. Or he could go on out to Idaho and dig for silver in style, maybe even hire some help to do the digging. One thing was certain; Jamison Jakes wouldn't have to worry about his next meal.

He began looking through the rest of the contents in the saddlebags, keeping items he considered to be important and tossing the rest. The only thing he wanted of Emory Gordon's was the money; from the Alamo Kid's bags he set aside the postal cards of the nude women which had provided entertainment for the Kid.

And from Daniel True's earthly possessions, Jakes kept the letters the old man had written to Elizabeth. As he was about to toss the letters in with the other gear to be packed away, he decided to read another, to try to know this man better, this Daniel True.

The envelope was dated August 13, 1869.

Jamison Jakes removed his spectacles, blew on them, rubbed the lenses with the end of the dresser cloth, replaced the glasses on his nose, and carefully opened the envelope.

As he read the words silently, Jakes could hear the voice of Daniel True:

My most precious Elizabeth,

I wish I were with you now, lying beside you perhaps, so I might consult with you. I have no one in whom I can confide, or even go to as a friend.

I am bothered, Elizabeth, more than at anytime in my life, except when I'd found I'd lost you. I have so much pain within me, and there the pain must stay, for it has no outlet.

Recently I killed a man. For sure, he was not a good man, and perhaps he deserved to die. But should it have been by my hand, for my profit?

You see, my delicate little flower, I have become a hunter of men as a means of livelihood. And now I have become a killer of men for the same reason.

I am now by profession what is called a "bounty hunter." Not a pretty name, I think, but very apt. When wolves kill cattle, ranchers pay a bounty for each wolf hide brought in. And desperate men, hungry men, go on the hunt and kill every wolf they find and collect the pay.

Instead of wolves, I hunt men who have reduced themselves to animals. I bring in their hides, dead or alive, and collect the bounty that's been placed on their heads.

All I had brought in had been alive, until that one who wouldn't go without a fight.

I can't begin to describe to you what it is I feel. I am sad, but not sorry. I don't feel any guilt because it was a fair fight and I came out the winner. I am angry more than anything. Angry that men turn bad and have to be hunted and sometimes killed. Angry that there is so much mistrust in the world that men have to wear guns and always be prepared to use them.

But so long as men are bad, there have to be men like me to provide the balance, the slight edge that keeps evil in check and a rein on anarchy.

What I do is not noble, but necessary.

Talking to you this way is always good for my soul. I yearn for companionship, some comrade who will listen to my woes and share theirs with me. I have no friend but you, Elizabeth, and even you don't know that.

Perhaps I have set the standards for close friendship too high for any person to meet. But someday it might happen. Then I will have someone to talk with about you, someone who will understand a man who is growing old holding onto a fading promise of happiness yet to be found.

That person must be somewhere, Elizabeth. When we meet, I will know. And then another person will know you.

Until then, please be tolerant of me by allowing me the privilege of our annual visit. You have soothed my troubled spirit for now.

Your thankful servant and friend,

Daniel

A large lump had grown in the throat of Jamison Jakes by the time he finished reading the letter. He slowly read each word twice more. As he folded the paper and returned it to the envelope, he asked the question, "Why me, Daniel? Damn you, why me?"

A new problem now faced Jamison Jakes: he had to get from Cheyenne to somewhere in Indiana and find a woman who may not even be living and tell her something, with no idea what. He knew with another hard winter on its way, he couldn't make the trip on horseback. The stagecoach would be faster, and somewhat warmer, but still cold. A man of means going on a long trip should not have to be cold, even in winter.

Jakes headed for the train station. Once there, he sought help from the station master in seeing if he could get a train to a town called Lawrence, Indiana.

"That's a new one on me," he said. "But let me check the book."

It would take a few minutes of leafing through pages of a large master schedule before the question could be answered. While he waited, Jakes studied a map on the wall showing all the railroad routes in the country. Only a few were in place for the states and territories west of the Mississippi River, but to the east the map looked like a spider's web. He was especially interested in what had happened with rail service in Kentucky. Many lines had been added since he had left home.

"Here we go," the man announced with pride. "I found Lawrence. It's about twenty miles outside Indianapolis."

"That's great," Jakes responded. "Write me up a ticket for there."

"Well, as close as I can get you is Indianapolis, but the schedule shows you can get a stage from there out to Lawrence."

A train would be leaving Cheyenne at noon for Omaha. From there he would need to switch to another train and go to either Chicago or St. Louis. From either of these cities he could go straight to Indianapolis with only a few stops in between.

"I can write you up a ticket all the way to Indianapolis," the station master said with great pride. "But you got to decide which direction you want to go out of Omaha"

"Just give me a ticket to Omaha," Jakes said, "I'll decide when I get there which way I want to go."

"Cost you more that way," said the disappointed station master. "A ticket straight through to Indianapolis is a heap cheaper."

"That's okay," Jakes said. "Sometimes I like to pay more just to keep my options open."

Jamison Jakes had a lot to do in the few hours before he was to leave. He sold his horse and saddle to the livery owner and his rifle to the man who ran the hardware store. He bought a carpet-bag valise and transferred the remaining contents of the saddlebags into it, then tossed the weather-beaten bags. There was room in the bottom of the valise for the coffee pot and tin cup and plate he had carried with him since his time in the war. He tied his bed roll securely to the handles of the bag, then fashioned a money belt of sorts from two bandannas and tied it around his waist, under his long johns, after taking one of the hundred-dollar bills to the bank to be broken into smaller denominations of gold and silver.

He wasn't sure if there would be anything to eat on the train, so after a shave and haircut he went to the general store and bought a loaf of sourdough bread and a wheel of cheese. He made the rounds to say goodbye to the few people he thought could have become good friends if he'd stayed in town long enough, then hauled his luggage and food to the depot to wait.

The train, arriving on time, was a curious sight. Only one car, located directly behind the engine, was for passengers. Following were three empty cattle cars, a couple of half-loaded freight cars, and a caboose with a red lantern hanging outside the back door. The passenger car had a wood stove in the middle, a small relief room at one end, and three coal oil lamps hanging on pegs. Firewood was stacked near the stove.

Jamison Jakes' fellow travelers were an equally curious lot.

He noticed the elderly woman first. She was so small that she couldn't see over the seat in front of her and her hair was as white as the snow that was falling from the dark Wyoming sky. Her lap was covered with the large gray and black afghan she was knitting. Her little fingers moved with such smoothness and precision that it seemed to Jakes she was more machine than woman. She looked up and saw him staring at her, and her eyes smiled; then he knew she was much more than a knitting machine. She was someone's mother, he thought, maybe someone's grandmother, who had promised a new bed throw or lap warmer to be delivered at the end of her trip. She only had time to glance up from her work and smile with her eyes.

Jakes' attention shifted to a large man sitting alone in the front of the car. Only the back of his massive head could be seen, a head covered by a derby hat, a head that didn't move, a head that had two eyes that were either closed in sleep or riveted to the wall in front of him.

"A drummer," Jakes concluded. "Sells hardware."

A young Indian boy also sat alone near the front, reading a book in the dim light. Jakes took a seat next to the boy. There were other seats he could have taken, but seeing an Indian boy reading was enough to attract the attention of a man who had himself learned to read sitting at the feet of his mother.

Jakes squinted to read the title of the boy's book.

"The Pilgrim's Progress," said the boy.

"What?" asked a surprised Jamison Jakes.

"The Pilgrim's Progress," repeated the boy. "It's a great book. Have you read it?"

"Nope, can't say that I have. I don't read all that much. I learned some about the pilgrims, though. Studied 'em when I was a boy."

"This story isn't exactly about *the* pilgrims. It's about a pilgrim named Christian and a trip he took looking for heaven. Too bad you don't read much. My father says reading a good book is the best present a person can give himself."

"Well, do tell. That sure is a thick one. Think you'll ever get through it?"

"I've already read it twice."

"Whoa, you kiddin' me? How come you're readin' it again?"

"Each time, I learn something. I read it to learn, and to use that learning in my life."

"So what've you learned?" Jamison Jakes was feeling somewhat uneasy.

"Ignorance is bad. That's the main lesson I've learned from this book."

"You needed to learn that from a book?" Jamison Jakes had always known it wasn't smart to be stupid.

"Yes. In this story the pilgrim, Christian, goes on a journey from the City of Destruction to the Celestial City. The Celestial City is really heaven. The story is all about worthy companions and dreadful adversaries. In the end, both Christian and a fellow traveler named Ignorance arrive at their spiritual destination, but they won't let Ignorance into heaven. So, you see, ignorance is a bad thing."

Jamison Jakes at that moment was feeling pretty ignorant. He peered over the boy's shoulder to look at the dramatic illustrations.

"When you need a rest from your readin', do you think I might borrow the book for a spell?"

"You sure can, mister," the boy answered with some excitement. And if you have trouble with any of the words, I'll be glad to help. Someday I hope to be a teacher. I want all my tribe to be able to have the gift of learning secrets held in books."

The boy looked out the window for a long while before he spoke again. "We have so little of anything else. The white hunters have come in large numbers to our plains and forests and now the buffalo, deer, and antelope are almost gone, so we have little meat. The long-knives have chased us from our planting grounds and given the land to white settlers to farm or dig for gold or silver, so now we have no grain. We are given promises by Indian agents that are not kept and these agents even steal the food and blankets meant to be ours in exchange for all that the white man has been taken from us."

"How do you manage to get by?" Jakes asked, feeling slightly guilty that his plan not long ago had been to mine for silver or raise cattle on land that had once been farmed by others who were now displaced.

"We survive by taking cattle from the ranchers and grain from the farmers. My father and other men from the tribe go in the night and steal so the women and children will not die from starvation. The men, in turn, are hunted down and, when caught, they are shot or hanged. My father says that for every brave who is killed, three children die from starvation."

Jakes felt his guilt turn to anger. While driving the herd from the Dakotas, he had been in a party running after Indians who tried to make off with a few stray cows in the middle of the night. Once he was quite sure he had shot and killed one of the thieves and had basked for a while in the glow of the other wranglers' cheers and back slaps.

"My God," Jakes said half-aloud. "I might've killed three children."

"What's that, Mister?" asked the boy.

"Uh, nothin'. Just thinkin'out loud, son. Just thinkin'." And then to change the subject, Jakes asked, "Who's your father?"

"He is called Nerak and he's the chief of our tribe. As his oldest son, I will someday be chief."

Nerak! That was the renegade Daniel True had on his hunting list. Nerak! Who was thought to be nothing more than the savage leader of a band of savages but was clearly a man who valued education and wanted nothing more than a good life for his people. If Daniel had known the real story of why the Indians take from the ranchers, he would have done nothing to stop them. Jakes was sure of that.

"Where you headed, son?"

"I'm going to North Platte. The priest at the mission on our reservation is making it possible for me to go to their frontier seminary where I'll study in exchange for work. He has taught me much, but tells me there is more to be learned. I would not be going, but my father said this was something I must do for our people. I'll be there for two years."

The town's name suddenly made Jakes crave a good bottle of Platte River whiskey.

"How old are you?"

"I have passed my fifteenth summer. How old are you?"

"I've lived a heap more summers than that," Jakes

chuckled. "A heap more."

The two talked late into the evening. Jakes shared his bread and cheese with the boy and after another hour of small talk in the dark, they both fell asleep.

A jerk of the train woke Jakes with a start. He cleared his eyes and looked out the window just in time to see the depot sign passing by as the train picked up speed. The placard said NORTH PLATTE. The Indian boy was gone, but on the seat where he had sat next to Jakes, was a book. *The Pilgrim's Progress.*

Chapter 18

According to the printed schedule Jamison Jakes had been given at the station in Cheyenne, it would take another fourteen hours to reach Omaha. He looked around the car and realized that everyone except for him had gotten off in North Platte and no one had gotten on. After stoking the stove and adding more wood, he cut a large piece of bread and broke off a hunk of cheese for his breakfast. As he ate, he stared at the bleak Nebraska landscape as the train rolled through it. He'd spent a great deal of time in Nebraska after leaving the wagon train in central Kansas; he didn't care much for the place, but there was always a need for short-term help on a farm or ranch. He had determined Nebraska had only three colors: green in the springtime, white in the winter and brown the rest of the time. It was in its brown season now, with a few patches of white in the hills.

To help time pass, Jakes tried to recall all the jobs he had held since he had quit the scouting business. He'd punched cows on six different spreads; helped sow wheat for two farmers; assisted in harvesting wheat for three farmers; butchered hogs; herded sheep; cut and stacked hay; helped string fifty miles of fence line; cleared land; raised barns; helped build houses; plowed ground and planted potatoes; plowed ground and planted corn; dug holes to plant an apple orchard; cleaned horse stalls in livery stables; rode shotgun for Wells Fargo; swept out saloons in exchange for drinks; and, finally, went on the payroll of the Cheyenne Stock Growers Association.

"It's about time I stopped driftin' and settled down," he thought.

Up to this point he didn't have the wherewithal to do any settling, but now with the Widowmaker's loot he could give serious consideration to doing just about anything he wanted. His first impulse, after realizing he was a wealthy man, had been to buy a small spread and raise breeding stock. However, after more pondering on that idea, he had all but abandoned it. Dealing with any kind of animal to make a living was hard; and always a gamble. He had seen good men give it a try, work their asses off twelve hours a day, and still go under. His thinking now was he would be happier owning a general store or livery stable where the hours were set and the business steady. It was good to have options.

As the train clacked along, Jakes picked up the gift the Indian boy had left him. It was the biggest book he had ever opened. There was no way, he thought, he would he ever read it all. He started the journey by leafing through the pages looking at the pictures, hoping he could get the gist of the story without having to read a lot. The illustrations were helpful, but not sufficient to satisfy his growing curiosity about the plot. Had he not been captive to a slow-moving train with no one to talk to and nothing to do except count telegraph poles as they passed by the window, he might have found easier ways to occupy his time.

Getting started was the hardest part, but after just a few

pages he was hooked. Reading had never held much truck with Jakes. It wasn't that he couldn't read or understand the meaning of words, but that it was such a passive activity. He could never sit still in one place for very long. Now that he had nothing to do but sit, he was glad for the book.

He soon realized that he, like Christian, was a pilgrim. But he wasn't searching for heaven, just some peaceful place he could call home. In trying to find that spot, he had gone through many trials and tribulations. He recalled people in the past with whom he could identify as characters in the story: Obstinate, Hypocrisy, Mistrust, Ignorance, and Apollyon, the destroyer. He had come across far more of these types in his life than the nice ones: Evangelist, Goodwill, Interpreter, and Faithful.

"Hey," Jakes said to himself when he closed the book to rest his eyes, "this is pretty good stuff."

The train stopped every fifty miles or so to take on water and wood for the boiler. At each stop there was a telegraph shack with coffee and an operator eager to talk. The telegraphers were always on duty in case there were emergencies to report or receive. This was a lonely and dangerous existence, Jakes concluded, and mentally checked that job off his list of occupations he might do once he found his own peaceful place.

When Jamison Jakes arrived in Omaha, it was dark and the train depot was just closing. He caught the station master as he was locking the door and asked about getting to Indianapolis.

"They's two ways a-getting' there," he responded. "One is to be on board the nine-fifteen in the mornin' for Chicago; the other is to take the three o'clock afternoon run to St. Louis. The St. Louis route is a mite longer over the long haul, but you'd have to hog-tie me to get me to go back to Chicago. Fare to St. Louie is higher, but that run has a sleeper car. 'Course, they's an extra charge if you decide to use the sleeper."

Jakes thanked the man and said he'd decide by morning which way to go.

"Well, if you're takin' the run to Chicago, be back in plenty of time. There won't be no waitin' for stragglers."

The mention of sleep reminded Jakes it'd been several days since he'd seen a bed, so he checked into a small hotel across from the station, got a steak in the café next door, went to bed without undressing, and fell asleep with the large book resting on his chest.

It was fortunate that Jakes had decided the night before that he would go to Indianapolis through St. Louis. When he woke it was after ten o'clock, and the train for Chicago had already gone. When he did arrive at the train station and had bought his ticket a little after noon, Jakes had time to walk about and see some of the sights of Omaha. He paid the station master two bits to stow his valise, which now contained his Colt revolver. Wearing guns inside the city limits had been outlawed and the last thing Jakes wanted to do was get locked up in this busy town and have to stay one minute longer than it was necessary.

Omaha was about the size of Denver, but seemed much bigger. People scurried in and out of shops and tall buildings; street vendors were on every corner; horse-drawn trolleys ran on tracks going both directions up and down the broad avenues; buggies had to park in special lots where drivers had to pay a fee; and saddle horses were nowhere to be seen.

After less than an hour, Jakes returned to the station, claimed his valise, found a seat, and pulled out his book. He was very glad he had not chosen to go to Chicago.

The trip from Omaha to St. Louis was long but uneventful. He paid an extra two dollars to get a bunk bed in the sleeper car and was glad for that. This train also had a café car where coffee, hard-boiled eggs and wrapped sandwiches could be bought. The weather had warmed some and the windows could be cracked open a little for better air circulation. Jakes was impressed with the contrast between this way of traveling and wagon trains.

He also had time for reading. Before the train pulled into St. Louis he had finished Part One of *The Pilgrim's Progress.*

Chapter 19

The train route from St. Louis to Indianapolis, while direct, was less than speedy with many stops along the way. Jamison Jakes was constantly amazed by the number of small towns. Much of southern Illinois had been divided and subdivided into hundreds of farms, teeming with vast fields of corn, cabbage, beets, carrots, and potatoes. Pig farms were evident by their smell. Large chicken houses were everywhere with signs painted on their sides touting leghorns or Plymouth rocks or Rhode Island reds as being the "best chickens in the world." There were no steers to be seen, but instead large herds of dairy cows had worn paths between the pastures and the barns. Goats and sheep were fewer in number but maintained a presence, nonetheless.

All of these farm operations were sustained by the small and numerous commercial centers dotting the region. Every town had placed itself alongside the tracks and the train stopped at each one to take on or leave off passengers, produce, supplies and mail. This made for slow progress between the major cities.

150

Among all of his home-school studies, Jamison Jakes' favorite had been history. He had not kept up with much of what had gone on in the country since his school days, but up to that time he had memorized the names of all the American presidents, in the order in which they had served, and had tried to learn as much about each of them as he could. His favorite president had been Andrew Jackson of Tennessee, mainly because Jackson was a tough frontiersman. The president who Jakes knew almost nothing about was Abraham Lincoln. Lincoln had just begun his presidency, and had moved into the White House, in March of the year Jakes ran off to enlist.

He did know that Lincoln had made Springfield his home before becoming president. Jakes wanted to know more about this man, and the scheduled three-hour layover in Springfield would provide him with the perfect opportunity.

At the train station, for twenty cents and a one-dollar refundable deposit, passengers could rent a padlock and key and secure their belongings in a wooden locker. Jakes opted for this service, and stepped out into the chilly afternoon air.

At one end of the platform, encased in glass, was a plat of the city of Springfield showing the location of the statehouse and the home and former law offices of Abraham Lincoln. Since all were within walking distance of the train station, Jakes made a mental note of their locations and started trekking.

Lincoln had made Springfield his home for twenty-four years and lived in the same house for the last seventeen before being elected President. Jake's stroll took him there first. In this home, Lincoln was a husband, father, politician, and President-elect. The house was not a mansion, which surprised Jakes, but it was a large two-story frame structure with fireplace chimneys on either end. A white picket fence sat atop a retaining wall designed to make possible a green level lawn. On a bronze plaque attached to the fence were the opening words of Lincoln's farewell remarks to the citizens of

Springfield, dated February 11, 1861:

> *My friends – No one, not in my situation, can appreciate my feeling of sadness at this parting. To this place, and the kindness of these people, I owe everything.*

A few blocks from the house Jakes discovered the downtown square. He searched for, and found, the Tinsley Building where Lincoln and his junior partner, William Herndon, rented office space on the third floor, facing the statehouse to the north. There were flyers in a wooden box outside the entrance explaining the area. In a black-bordered rectangle near the middle of the page were the words Lincoln spoke to Herndon as he was leaving for the White House: "If I live I'm coming back sometime, and then we'll go right on practicing law as if nothing had ever happened."

Jakes sat on a bench to read the remainder of the two-sided information sheet. A simple dateline showed the evolution of the Illinois capitals. The first capitol building was in Kaskaskia, which became a land-office town and the territorial capital in 1809. Next, Vandalia had become the second capital of Illinois in 1820, a couple of years after the state had joined the union, with the capitol housed in a simple two-story structure that was soon destroyed by fire. In 1824, Vandalia's second capitol was built to replace the one that burned. Much to the dislike of the citizens of Vandalia, in 1839 Illinois voters selected Springfield as the new state capital city, and in 1853 the new capitol building opened for business. By 1868 the state's economic and political growth placed so much demand on the existing facilities that construction for a new capitol was started. As a result, Jamison Jakes found himself looking at two massive edifices, although the one under construction appeared to be years from completion.

To the north of these sites, Jakes walked into a grove of elm trees that had been planted in a large square with each side about fifty feet in length. In the middle of the square was a small log cabin. A few people were milling about the grounds while others were leisurely going in and out the cabin door. A group of seven school-aged children and a woman were listening intently to a man in a guide uniform explaining this cabin was an exact replica of the Kentucky one in which Abraham Lincoln was born.

Jakes entered the cabin as two couples were leaving and, once inside, found himself alone. The building was a simple structure measuring no more than sixteen-by eighteen-feet and included one door and window, a stone fireplace and a dirt floor. Hanging in the center of the long back wall was a large picture of Lincoln as he must have appeared in the White House. On either side of the picture were framed copies of documents. Jakes looked closely at the shorter one entitled *The Gettysburg Address*, and then the longer one, with the heading *The Emancipation Proclamation*. Under Lincoln's picture was a statement declaring that these two acts had defined him as a man, a humanitarian, and a great president.

Jamison Jakes had heard of these documents, but didn't fully understand their significance. He had been fighting in Georgia when the battle of Gettysburg was waged and, although he was aware that the former slaves had been set free, he knew none of the details. He removed his spectacles and wiped the dust from the lenses with his shirt cuff so he could read more clearly. Since *The Gettysburg Address* was much shorter, Jakes started with that one, dated November 19, 1863.

> *Fourscore and seven years ago our fathers brought forth, upon this continent, a new nation, conceived in liberty and dedicated to the proposition that all men are created equal.*
>
> *Now we are engaged in a great civil war, testing whether that nation, or any nation so conceived and so dedicated, can long endure. We are met on a great battlefield of that war. We have come to dedicate a portion of it, as a*

*final resting place for those who died here, that
the nation might live. This we may, in all
propriety do. But in a larger sense we cannot
dedicate, we cannot consecrate, we cannot
hallow, this ground. The brave men, living and
dead, who struggled here, have hallowed it, far
above our poor power to add or detract. The
world will take little note, nor long remember
what we say here; while it can never forget what
they did here.*

*It is rather for us the living, we here be
dedicated to the great task remaining before us
– that from these honored dead we take
increased devotion to that cause for which they
here gave the last full measure of devotion –
that we here highly resolve that these dead shall
not have died in vain, that this nation shall have
a new birth of freedom, and that government of
the people, by the people, for the people shall
not perish from the earth.*

"Hey, that's really something," Jakes almost shouted, to the
giggles of the school children standing behind him.

He moved aside and quickly scanned the *Proclamation*;
grasping enough of its contents to get a feel for this official act
by which Lincoln freed the slaves. With his childhood passion
for history rekindled, Jakes vowed he'd locate a copy of this
document someday and study it carefully.

Time was nearing when the train would be leaving for
Indianapolis, so he quickened his step. This Springfield stop
had helped him gain a better understanding of some of the
circumstances of the war and, while he still had a problem
grasping his four-year involvement in it, he decided he was
glad his side had lost.

Jakes arrived at the station with just enough time to retrieve his valise from the locker and board the train. After a meal in the café car, he found his assigned bunk, thought for a bit about how he should proceed in finding Elizabeth once he got to Lawrence, and lapsed into a deep sleep.

When he awoke the train was sitting at the passenger platform in Indianapolis.

Chapter 20

Jamison Jakes was immediately overwhelmed by the size of Indianapolis. He realized while passing through St. Louis that there were more people in the world than he ever imagined; because of that he had stayed on the train during the St. Louis layover. Now, in Indianapolis, he felt totally out of place. None of the men had cowboy hats and only a few wore boots. Women were in dresses with bustles, high-top laced shoes with three-inch heels, and hats with flowers all over them. There were a few men wearing large-brimmed straw hats and a fewer number of women with sun bonnets; these were farmers and farmer's wives Jakes assumed.

His train had come in from the west. Now two others sat at the station on each side of the large depot, one facing north and the other south.

Thankfully, Indianapolis was not his final destination. He was headed for Lawrence, and the sooner he got there, the less uncomfortable he'd feel. Getting there proved to be as simple as buying a ticket from the Wells Fargo stagecoach office and waiting for the stage to pull out.

The trip to Lawrence was scheduled to take almost four hours, covering just eighteen miles. Looking at the route map, Jakes couldn't figure why the time didn't equate with the distance. In just a short while he understood. The traffic was unbelievable throughout the city. Long lines of wagons hauling freight and produce, buggies of various sizes and shapes, and numerous pushcarts clogged every street. At intersections, blue-clad policemen were trying to establish and maintain some semblance of order by stopping the progress on one street to allow passage from the other.

The stage itself was a type that Jakes hadn't seen. Rather than two seats facing each other with leg room in between, this coach had five bench seats, all facing forward and providing little room for legs or anything else. Passengers could get on and off at a number of "stage stop" locations along the route, with the driver announcing the next stop in a loud, booming voice.

By the time "Lawrence – end of the line" was bellowed, there were only three passengers remaining: Jakes and two women who had been on board since the third stop in Indianapolis. He had taken a seat on the back row where there seemed to be a bit more leg room with the women immediately in front of him.

On impulse, Jakes opened his valise and took out the picture of Elizabeth. "Excuse me ladies," he said politely, "could you take a look at this picture and tell me if you might recognize this girl? She'd be maybe twenty years older now and she'd be livin' with a husband and most likely a kid or two."

The women studied the photograph and soon one said, "You know, Bessie, that could well be the egg lady who lives out of town a piece and raises all those chickens. Though I've never seen her with a man or child, it's a good likeness. Yep, that might well be her."

Bessie was not so quick to agree, but conceded the possibility.

Mixed feelings of relief and anxiety made Jakes' pulse race. Could it be the search was almost over? But now if he'd found the woman, what would he say to her? His anger toward Elizabeth had assuaged a great deal since leaving Cheyenne, so yelling at her no longer seemed viable. When the moment arrived that he and she met face to face, he hoped he would find the right words.

"Thank you kindly, ladies," Jakes said while retrieving the picture. "Can't tell you how glad I'll be to find this gal. We lost track of her when she moved up here from Tennessee."

"Oh, my," Bessie said in an apologetic tone. "Then I'm afraid that can't be the egg lady; she's lived here all her life."

Jakes was in a stew as to what his next moves should be. He'd made up his mind that he would spend no more than five days in Lawrence looking for Elizabeth, and then head back. But back to where? Cheyenne? The Idaho Panhandle? Make for Dakota Territory and wait out the winter until the round-up starts? At least there was no need to look for work; what was left of the Widowmaker's loot would last a long time if he was careful with his spending. He suddenly decided that having too many options may be worse than having none.

Lawrence offered two choices for lodging. One was a fancy-looking three-story hotel with a large lobby and adjoining café. The other was Pioneer Village, a series of twelve small log buildings a few blocks off the main street. The cabins formed a square, three to a side. Each structure contained a bed, a table, two upright chairs, a large bowl and pitcher, a towel and washcloth hanging from hooks, a bar of soap, a coal oil lamp, two large candles, and a cook stove for both heat and boiling water. A teakettle sat on the stove. The outhouse was handily located, and there was a water pump in the center of the square. The door to each cabin had a small opening in the top panel that could be locked closed or be opened to let air in. There was no window. Jakes signed up for cabin #7, put Elizabeth's picture in his pocket, hid the valise under the bed, locked the door, and made his way back to the town center.

As he walked, he developed a simple search strategy. He would go to all the places in town where women usually spend time and show Elizabeth's picture around until someone recognized her.

He started with the general store. A very pleasant clerk looked at the tintype for a long minute and said, "That sure looks a heap like the woman I get my eggs from, but I couldn't say for certain. Her name's Stella Olson." Jakes thanked him and explained that the woman in the picture had moved to Indiana from Tennessee. "Nope, the egg lady wouldn't be her then. She's always lived in these parts." Jakes just nodded.

His next stop was the post office. As the woman behind the counter studied the picture, but before she could speak, Jakes assured her the woman in the photo wasn't the egg lady. "Well, shucks, I was just getting' ready to say that's who I thought it might be," the woman said disappointedly. "I can't imagine then who she is. Sorry."

As Jakes neared the door on his way out, he noticed a stack of newspapers on a shelf, copies of a publication called *The Lawrence Town Crier*. He took one and returned to the woman behind the counter.

"How often is your newspaper printed?" he asked.

"Comes out about every other week, dependin' on how long it takes for Charlie Cobb, the editor, to get enough advertisements lined up to pay for it. Charlie gives the paper away for free and just makes it run on the ads."

"Where's the office?"

"Two blocks down, then just 'round the corner to the right."

Jakes found the newspaper office without difficulty; however, the door was locked and a sign in the window posted the open hours of seven o'clock in the morning until one o'clock in the afternoon.

Jakes had hit upon a new plan. He would buy an advertisement in the next issue of Mr. Cobb's paper and run the picture of Elizabeth for all to see. A fifty-dollar reward would be offered to anyone who could identify her and tell him where she could be found. Then all he need do was wait in cabin #7 at Pioneer Village and listen for a knock on the door.

It was getting near dusk and Jakes realized he hadn't had a decent meal in days. He was too rail-weary and dirty to go to the café, so he returned to the general store and picked up a package of dried fruit, a box of crackers, and a small sack of coffee to see him through until morning. He would eat an early breakfast out and be at the newspaper office the minute it opened.

There was a smell of rain in the air when Jakes reached his cabin and a cold breeze was blowing from the east. He quickly lit the lamp, built a fire, filled the large pitcher and teakettle with water from the pump, went to the outhouse, came back inside and began to settle in for the night. His coffee pot and cup were in the bottom of his valise, so he pulled the bag from its hiding place under the bed.

Rummaging through its contents, he came across the packet of Daniel True's letters and the copy of *The Pilgrim's Progress*. His intention to read more of the book while on the train had been good, but not fulfilled. He placed the book back in the valise, putting it on top of everything so it would be handy, just in case he needed to bide his time.

While waiting for the coffee water to boil, Jakes stripped down to his long johns, mumbled something about how dirty they had gotten, and picked up the letter bundle. He had made up his mind, after reading the first five missives, that he wouldn't read any others. They were so personal, so private, that he felt like someone hiding in the shadows and peeping into the window of a man's soul. He lit one of the candles and spread the letters out in front of it, alongside the picture of Elizabeth -- a small memorial to Daniel True.

As Jakes sat on his bed, sipping coffee, he wondered how this trip would end. He felt a bit of pride in himself for traveling so far and making an honest effort to carry out his friend's dying wish. This part would end soon, one way or another. What then?

The candle was flickering, and when Jakes bent over to blow it out, he noticed something: there were three envelopes that he hadn't seen before. Instead of having dates on them, they were marked simply "One," "Two," and "Three".

Jakes poured what was left of the hot water from the teakettle into the wash bowl and scrubbed his hands and bearded face. Then he removed his long johns and the bandana-fashioned money belt he had worn since leaving Cheyenne and spot-washed the rest of his body. He put on his only pair of clean longjohns and turned down the bed.

Throughout his standing bath, Jakes had fought with his conscience. He was fine with not reading the other letters; but what about these new discoveries? They were probably not letters or they would be dated. Maybe they contained information that would be helpful in finding Elizabeth. Maybe they held money.

His conscience lost the fight.

Jamison Jakes, the ever-curious one, pulled a chair close to the fire, turned up the wick on the coal oil lamp and slowly opened the first envelope. Inside was a single piece of yellowed paper, folded in thirds. At the top was a heading "To Elizabeth from the Battlefield." There was no date.

> *How completely do I love you?*
> *So much that your pain is my pain,*
> *Your tears are my tears.*

> *The beating of your heart throbs in my chest.*
> *Through your eyes I see*
> *All that is beautiful.*
> *Through your words, my thoughts find life.*
> *Because you are lovely, I become lovely;*
> *Because you are strong, I find strength.*
> *How completely do I love you?*
> *So completely that I am no longer " I"*
> *But "we"*
> *And forever I am we, for we are one.*

Jakes sat stunned for a moment, realizing that he had once again intruded into the secret and personal life of his friend. But he wasn't sorry. He had discovered yet another side of the bounty hunter: Daniel True, poet.

Chapter 21

It was raining lightly when Jamison Jakes made his way in the morning darkness to a small café just across the street from the newspaper office. He had taken twenty dollars from his money belt before tying it back around his waist, so he could afford a large spread for breakfast. As he ate chicken-fried steak covered with gravy, potatoes and biscuits, and drank cup after cup of black coffee, he watched for a light to come on at the *Town Crier*. Exactly at seven o'clock, according to the coo-coo clock hanging on the café wall, a figure stood at the newspaper office door and soon a lamp was burning inside.

As Jakes entered the office, a bell attached to the door rang and a man came from a back room carrying a bucket load of coal.

"Be right with you as soon as I get a fire going," the man announced. "The nights are getting longer and the days are getting colder; winter will be here before we know it." As he talked he twisted what appeared to be old newspapers into tight cylinders and used them to kindle the fire in the large potbellied stove. Once he had added a half bucket of coal to the flames, he closed the stove door and rubbed his hands together.

"Now, sir," he said, smiling at Jakes, "what can I do for you?"

"Are you Mister Cobb?" Jakes knew full well the man had to be the editor, Charlie Cobb, but he wanted the man to know that he knew his name.

"Yep, everybody calls me Charlie, though. Don't like to think I'm old enough yet to be called Mister Cobb."

"Charlie, my name's Jamison Jakes and I'd like to take out an ad in your paper. That is, if you plan to print another issue real soon."

"Wish I could tell you when that'll be. With winter coming on, the merchants slow way down in their advertising and it usually doesn't pick up again until the Christmas season. I've got a few regulars, like the general store and the bank, but they don't buy a lot of space."

"How much more space do you need to fill before you can print?"

"I'm about a half-page short. If I can find four clients who will take an eighth each, I'll be able to put her to bed right away. All the news stories and features are set, assuming the news doesn't get too old."

"I'll take the half page, Charlie, if you can get the paper printed and out by tomorrow morning."

"Well, sir, that's a pretty tall order but, if I get started right away, and if you're willing to lend a hand, I think we can make it. What is it you sell?"

"Not sellin', just lookin' for someone I need to find real quick."

Jamison Jakes and Charlie Cobb stood at the counter and drank coffee while Jakes related some of the story of Daniel True and Elizabeth, without mentioning their names or the fact that Elizabeth had come from Tennessee, and of Jakes' travels from Wyoming to Indiana in search of the woman. Jakes shared his idea of offering a fifty-dollar reward to anyone who could help him find Elizabeth. They decided that the half-page ad should be made up to look something akin to a wanted poster, with enough information given to interest people in the search but not so much that it wouldn't allow Jakes to question those persons about the woman's name and where she had lived before coming to Lawrence, to determine it was truly her.

Cobb expressed some concern about being able to make a gravure plate from the tintype photograph. He had the equipment and the necessary chemicals, but had very little experience in using them. Jakes only comment was "What the hell, Charlie, let's give it a try."

While Cobb began the picture reproduction process, Jakes sat with pen and paper to design the ad. After a few tries that ended in the waste basket, he was finally satisfied.

INFORMATION WANTED
$50.00 REWARD
DO YOU KNOW THIS WOMAN?
(picture goes here, Charlie)
SHE IS NOW TWENTY YEARS OLDER THAN THIS PICTURE
ANYONE WITH GOOD INFORMATION
GET IN TOUCH WITH JAMISON JAKES
IN CABIN #7
AT THE PIONEER VILLAGE
BEFORE SIX O'CLOCK THIS FRIDAY
NOTE: YOU MAY THINK THIS WOMAN IS STELLA OLSON, THE EGG LADY, BUT SHE ISN'T

Cobb thought the copy looked fine and that it told the story. A few customers came and went during the morning, slowing their work some. At one o'clock Cobb hung a "Closed for the Day" sign on the door and the two men walked across the street for a bite of lunch. If Cobb had done the gravure process correctly, the plate would be ready by four, and the press could begin an hour later. After their lunch was finished, Jakes said he needed a walk and promised to be back at the office to see the proof of the ad at four.

The heavier rain that had been falling earlier was now reduced to a fine mist but the east wind still carried a nip. Parts of Daniel True's poem to Elizabeth kept repeating themselves in Jakes' mind, not unlike hearing a catchy tune and having no control over its playing over and over. His walk had no designed plan. He entered most of the stores on the main street, looking around at the merchandise with no intention of buying anything. He studied carefully the face of every woman he met; thinking one of them might be Elizabeth. To the few whom he felt could possibly be, he tipped his hat and asked politely, "Excuse me ma'am, could I trouble you to tell me your name?" Of those who responded, none was called Elizabeth.

A few minutes before four, Jakes rapped on the door of the *Town Crier* office and was let in by a very excited Charlie Cobb. "Woo, doggies, Jamison! I got it to work. We're going to be able to print the picture!" Jakes thought if the Alamo Kid had been there at that moment, he would have said, "Well ain't that a wonderment!"

Cobb assured Jakes that he would print the paper during the night and have the two boys he hired for distribution get them out first thing in the morning. Walking back to his cabin, Jakes stood for a few minutes looking through the window of a saloon. It had been a long, dry trip; he needed a drink. The thought of coming this distance and not finding Elizabeth was discouraging; he deserved a drink. The mixed aroma of whiskey and beer coming from the saloon lured him through the door; he wanted a drink. Once inside, his whiskey-deprived saliva glands began to flow. He turned and quickly left; he knew he couldn't have a drink.

Chapter 22

For the first night in so many, Jamison Jakes slept soundly. Travel fatigue, combined with relief that a good plan to locate Elizabeth was in motion, had slowed his body and mind to a pace that allowed slumber to catch up. Jakes knew from the amount of light coming under the cabin door that it was full daylight. Rain drops were bouncing on the roof. Because he was eager to see the advertisement in the *Town Crier*, Jakes decided that his first activity of the day was to locate a copy. He splashed water on his face, quickly dressed, and headed for the *Town Crier* office. As soon as he reached the main street, he saw the paper had already been distributed. Many early-risers were reading it while eating breakfast in the hotel café. Some were using it for an umbrella as they scurried along the boardwalks, while others had theirs folded under their arms. Jakes stepped inside the post office and picked up a copy.

"Holy Mary," Jakes said to no one in particular, "would you look at that!" The Elizabeth ad covered the entire bottom half of the front page. It couldn't be missed by anyone who even casually picked up the *Crier*. Jakes quickened his step to the paper's office and found Charlie Cobb locking the door to leave.

"Hey, Charlie! Thanks for puttin' my ad on the front page; I sure didn't expect that."

"Think nothing of it. That's the first half-pager I ever sold, so I sure didn't want it to be overlooked."

"Let me buy you some breakfast."

"Very kind of you, but I was here all night printing and I'm bushed. And you'd best get back to your place. Who knows, that woman may be knocking on your door as we speak."

"My Lord, you're right."

"How long will you be in town?"

"I'll wait two full days. If I haven't found her by then, chances are I never will."

"That makes sense. Let me know how things turn out."

"Sure will, Charlie, and thanks again."

Instead of taking time to eat breakfast, Jakes made a quick stop at the general store and bought bread, cheese, and a tin of peaches. Nothing too fancy, but they would be filling.

As Charlie Cobb had predicted, there was a woman, with a man, waiting on the porch of the little cabin. Jakes unlocked the door and asked them in. As the centerpiece of his plan, Jakes had decided to invite in everyone who came to the door in answer to the ad. Listening to their stories, he would be alert to any clue that might let him know if they really did know Elizabeth. Two facts would remain unknown to the visitors: Elizabeth's name and that she had been raised in Tennessee.

By the end of the day, Jakes had listened to five different persons claiming they were certain the woman in the photograph was, respectively, an aunt, a childhood friend, a girl who had visited for a couple of weeks several months before, the wife of a former circuit-riding preacher, and a woman who died ten years before and could be found in the local cemetery.

There were no Elizabeths.

Long after dark set in, a steady rain was falling and Jakes had to run with his mackinaw over his head to get to the outhouse without being drenched. Fortunately there was enough water in the pitcher to make a pot of coffee, so he didn't need to stand at the pump in the rain. He built a fire, shivering a bit in the dampness of the cabin, but soon the wood was blazing and crackling and coffee water was boiling. He pulled off his boots and wet shirt and put them on a chair near the fire to dry.

He cut thick slices of bread and cheese with the skinning knife, used the knife to punch a large hole in the tin of peaches, and then tossed the instrument back into the valise. He poured the peach syrup into his cup and sipped it slowly, pretending it was Platte River whisky, and then began his feast.

For a brief moment as he ate he considered starting Part Two of *The Pilgrim's Progress*, even going so far as to take it out of the carpet bag and place it on the bed. But in doing so, his eye caught sight of the loose envelopes with "One," "Two," and "Three" written on them. Knowing what number One had contained, he was more than curious about the other two.

With a sense of reverence Jakes slowly tore the end from the envelope. The paper inside was less yellowed than the first. At the top of the sheet Daniel had written, "A sleepless night somewhere in Nebraska." And then, "Thoughts on Eternity." Daniel True had written another poem.

> *I lie alone in my sepulcher, eyes open and*
> *seeing not.*
> *My poor ears strain to gather in any sound*
> *of murmuring life above me.*
> *But there are no sounds here so far beneath*
> *the sod,*

for there are none above who speak.
My silent voice screams at ears that are not.
I am alone with me.
Alone with me again: such a death.
Sepulcher
on earth I am within myself, remembering
Such a short life lived so long ago.
But that was when I was outside my tomb,
Breathing the sun, watching the moon
through
the branches of a lonely pine, seeing
streams in the desert, and loving
to the fullest with a woman named Love.
Such a short life lived so long ago
Now I return to myself, my crypt.
Within myself I see not nor hear
and have no desire to do either.
For there are no ears to hear a soundless
voice.
So with the world spinning, stopping, and
spinning again,
I, within myself, my eternity, think on a
short life lived so long ago.

Jamison Jakes let his hands fall limp into his lap as he tried to understand what he had just read. Is it possible for a man to be so lonely, so broken-hearted, that he would consider his life to be over while still living?

Jakes was starting to read the poem again when a knock sounded. Jakes quickly unlatched the small door in the upper panel and saw a bearded man, rain running from the brim of his hat onto his face.

"What can I do for you?" Jakes asked.

"You the man looking to find that woman from the newspaper?"

"Yep, that's me."

"I know who she is and I can take you right to her."

"Just a second, I'll unlock the door."

Once inside, the man stood in front of the stove and briskly rubbed his hands together to warm them quickly. "Is it for sure you're givin' a fifty-dollar reward for findin' this woman?" the man asked.

"That's right. What can you tell me about her?"

The stranger suddenly reached into the pocket of his jacket, pulled out a single-shot derringer pistol, and pointed it at Jakes.

"I know that she's goin' to earn me fifty dollars," the man said with a crooked smile. "So if you'll just hand it over, I'll be on my way."

Jakes mind raced with thoughts of what would happen when the man was given the money. He couldn't leave Jakes alive to report the theft and identify the thief. The small .32 caliber derringer report would not be heard over the rain storm. The man would be miles away before Jakes' body would be discovered. There seemed to be no other conclusion. The man would kill him.

"I been thinkin', too, that if you got fifty dollars to give away, you must have a heap more. So let's just have that along with the reward money."

"You're right; I do have more – a lot more. But it isn't here; I have it hidden in the woods just outside of town. I'll take you to it and you can have it all if you promise not to hurt me. Just give me time to put on a dry shirt."

Jakes went to the open valise sitting on the bed. Inside the bag, right on top where he had tossed it, was the Widowmaker's skinning knife. Jakes grasped the handle firmly in his palm, and spinning to the right, threw the knife underhanded as hard as he could in the direction of the scruffy intruder. The man screamed in pain and Jakes heard the derringer go off. He knew immediately he wasn't shot.

The man was on the floor, the knife sticking from his thigh. A pool of blood had already begun to form. Jakes pulled the knife from the leg and held it to the man's throat.

"I should go ahead and finish you off," Jakes said angrily.

But instead, he dragged the bleeding crook to the door, opened it, and shouted into the night for help.

Chapter 23

It took most of what was left of the night to clear up all the trouble the thief had caused. A neighbor in cabin #4 had responded to Jamison Jakes' shouts for help and rode his horse bareback to summon the sheriff. Two deputies responded in short order. The bleeding man was handcuffed and put in the back of a lock-up wagon to be taken, first to the doctor's office to get the knife wound stitched, then on to jail. The deputies left a form for Jakes to complete, along with a lead pencil, asking him to explain in as much detail as possible what had occurred. He was told to bring the form by the sheriff's office and have a talk with the law man in the morning.

The form appeared simple enough and the instructions at the bottom said to write on the back if more space was needed. The first information item requested was "Name." He had no trouble with that.

The next two lines, however, were very perplexing: "Place of Residence" and "Mailing Address." After a long period of staring at the form, Jakes wrote "Lexington, Kentucky" to answer the residence question. During the many long hours and days since leaving Cheyenne, he had thought a great deal about returning to his place of birth, getting a steady job, and replanting his roots. There had to be people still around he would know, and who would know him. Lexington, although his family had never lived in town, was becoming more and more an option, if not the only option.

Providing the mailing address information was impossible, however. Since leaving home to join the army, Jamison Jakes never had a permanent address. The truth be out, in his thirty-four years of existence he had neither mailed nor received a letter of any kind. He wrote on the line "None" and sat transfixed looking at the word. Eighteen years, more than half his lifetime, had been spent wandering about in his own world, answering to no one but himself. Eighteen years of odd jobs and no jobs, of being hot and dirty in the summer and cold and dirty in the winter, of never being cared for in sickness, of having no one but himself to laugh with – or to cry with.

Suddenly the words of his poet friend found meaning. He reread Daniel True's thoughts about loneliness and realized that his body was, like True's, his sepulcher – his tomb. This realization made him shudder and once again to crave a bottle of whiskey.

Sleep never found its way that night to Jamison Jakes' bed. He finished writing the report for the sheriff before dawn and drank coffee until daylight finally came. His only thought for the day was to tie up whatever loose ends still dangled and get out of town. The promise of staying another day with hope of finding Elizabeth was made only to himself and, in passing, to Charlie Cobb, so it could be easily broken. No doubt there would be others who might try to claim the reward, but Jakes had lost faith that Elizabeth would ever be found.

He spent the better part of an hour with the sheriff and signed an affidavit swearing what he had written in the report was the way everything had happened. This would be used as evidence in the thief's trial and Jakes wouldn't have to stay around to appear in court.

He needed food and wanted to say goodbye to Charlie Cobb so he headed for the café across from the *Town Crier* office. As he ate his breakfast, he could see Charlie moving around behind the counter. People were coming and going in and out the office door. Cobb was a very busy man this morning.

When he finished breakfast, Jakes waited until a woman customer had exited the office and Charlie Cobb was alone, and then went inside. Cobb looked both startled and pleased to see him.

"Hey, Jamison! Man, did you ever have a night of it! Folks are talking this morning of nothing else but about how you almost got robbed and how you went up against a gun with only a knife and still came out the winner."

"Well, Charlie," Jakes chuckled, "that's what happened all right. But it was a real small gun and a real big knife."

"I don't know what luck you had yesterday with finding your woman, but I've had a steady stream of people through here this morning trying to get more information than was in the ad. I guess they wanted to see if I could be of any help to them before they looked you up. Fifty dollars is a lot of money around here. I told them I didn't know any more than they did."

"Did any say who they thought the woman might be?"

"They all did, and I wrote down what they told me."

"Could you show me what you wrote?"

"Sure thing. Here're my notes."

It was easy for Jakes to know within seconds that none of these would pan out. The names given were Mabel, Dolly, Linda, Josephine, Wanda, Rebecca, and Annabelle. Not one Elizabeth. Jakes' deep sigh told Cobb everything.

"I'm sorry, Jamison."

"So am I, Charlie. I'm gonna be headin' out today soon as I get my things together. There's a stage into Indianapolis at noon and I plan to be on it."

"I'm sorry to hear that, but I really can't blame you. This town hasn't been too hospitable up to this point. Even so, it's a good place to live. Sure you won't stick around a spell and give us another chance?"

"You're a good man, Charlie," Jakes said with sincerity, "but the sooner I get gone, the sooner I'll get where I'm goin'."

"Where will that be?"

"Goin' back down to Kentucky, where I was born, and see if I can't find a life there. I'll tell you how to know if the woman I'm lookin' for pops up, and I'll trust you to keep that to yourself. When I get back down home, I'll telegraph you on how I can be reached. If you think for sure you've turned up the right woman, I'll come back with the reward money."

Jamison Jakes provided a few pieces of information, while not going into detail about Elizabeth and Tennessee and Daniel True, and Cobb said he had enough to go on.

They exchanged their goodbyes.

The stage from Lawrence to the rail station in Indianapolis left on schedule at noon and arrived four hours later, still on schedule. Jamison Jakes had no idea how he was to get from Indianapolis to Lexington, but found the depot ticket-master to be very helpful. Trains ran north and south through Indiana all the way to the Ohio River to a town called New Albany, just across the river from Louisville. Jakes could then reach the Louisville depot by either stage line or commuter train, whichever was more convenient. Two trains ran daily from Louisville to Lexington.

The most direct route between Indianapolis and New Albany was on the Wabash line, but there was a landslide on the Wabash, so the choices were a local train to Limedale or another to Bloomington, transferring at either stop to the

Monon which would take him directly into New Albany. The distance to Bloomington was shorter, but Jakes had passed through Limedale on the way from Springfield to Indianapolis and felt more comfortable going through a bit of territory he had already traveled, so he bought a ticket to New Albany through Limedale. Neither train would leave Indianapolis until morning: to Limedale at seven and Bloomington at eleven-thirty. The difference in time was due to the fact that it was the same Monon train that first went through Limedale then on to Bloomington. The sooner he could get out of Indianapolis, the better.

One advantage of being in a big city, or the only advantage that Jamison Jakes could think of, was the late hours the merchants kept. It was nearing six o'clock and only a handful of stores had closed. He considered briefly the possibility of spending the night in the train station, sleeping on a waiting-room bench. This was a natural inclination from his drifting days, when money was short and sleeping in barns or out in the open was the inexpensive way to travel. But he was a rich man now, with almost six-thousand dollars wrapped in bandannas tied around his waist.

He checked in at a hotel near the depot and went for a stroll to see if just possibly a barber shop might still be open. He was going to be back home in Kentucky in a couple of days and wanted to look as presentable as possible. There was a large basin in his room he was planning to use as a washtub for all his clothes, right down to the longjohns he had on. He stopped a man briefly to ask about a barber shop and was told there was one still open just around the next corner.

He would get a shave, have some dinner, then head back to the room and try to sleep. Jakes had a yearning for the days when he would kill time in a saloon. Nights when all he need do was go through those swinging doors, get a bottle, grab a table, and wile away the hours waiting for the fog to roll in.

When he found the barber shop, the lamps were still lit and only one man was sitting in a chair waiting his turn. Jakes entered the shop before he looked closely at the person in the white shirt holding the razor. The barber was a woman! Before the door had a chance to close behind him, he was back on the street, shaking his head, and went looking for steak and potatoes.

Chapter 24

To say that Jamison Jakes slept peacefully through the night would be to stretch the truth considerably. Against his will, he relived all that happened since leaving Cheyenne: the people he'd met, the train rides, the lessons he'd learned from an Indian boy and a poet, his almost getting killed trying to find Elizabeth, and his disappointment in not finding her. Then thoughts of the future invaded his mind: what he would do first when he reached Lexington, which childhood buddies he would try to find, the possibilities of what he might do with the Widowmaker's money, whether he would live in town or the country.

He still wanted a shave. His clothes were clean – somewhat damp, but at least clean. The woodstove fire had gone out during one of the few brief moments Jakes nodded off and he had counted on the heat to be his clothes dryer.

When he got to the station, the train conductor on the platform was yelling through a large megaphone, "All aboard for Limedale, with connections to Terre Haute and points west,

179

and to New Albany and points south!" Jakes had only enough time to dig his tin cup from his valise and have it filled with coffee by a woman working the lunch counter. His big meal the night before would have to tide him over for a while.

It occurred to Jamison Jakes that each time he sat on a train his mind went into high gear. Some thoughts were random, yet established some semblance of a pattern as they went along; others were concrete to the point of containing too much information and too many memories; others were a mixture of both, as he struggled to make some projection for what the future held. His life to now had seemed an unconnected series of events with no attempt to tie any two together. Every little while, the life he was living would end, and another would begin when he stopped in a new place for a few months – or weeks – or hours.

He had found some meaning in what he had been doing on this trip, this failed quest to find a woman who might not even exist. Lack of success in this venture, while disappointing, was still exhilarating in its own way. This was an act of friendship, an entirely new experience. He was fulfilling what he considered to be a sacred pledge to a dying friend. Now that pledge had been honored, or as well as he'd been able, and Jamison Jakes took pride in the realization that, for the first time, he had done something for someone with absolutely nothing expected in return.

The trip from Limedale to Bloomington on the Monon line was very pleasant. Large cornfields lay fallow and brown after the fall harvest. The only signs of life on farms that seemed to be everywhere were the domestic animals and the large numbers of deer foraging on what was left of the field crops after everything had been picked or cut.

Jakes was again lost in thought as he looked out the window, listening to the rhythmic "clickety-clack" of the wheels on the rails. Then, unexpectedly, the engine slowed to a crawl and blasted its whistle. The passengers began to mumble that the river must be over its bank again, causing the train to slow down as it passed over the trestle and through the water. Jamison Jakes lowered the window next to his seat and stuck his head out to see. While he couldn't get a view of the water causing the slowdown, he did see a large billboard along the track that read

WELCOME TO LAWRENCE COUNTY INDIANA
THE LIMESTONE CAPITAL OF THE WORLD

It took a full minute for it to sink in. Lawrence County, Indiana. Lawrence *County*! Could this possibly be the place Elizabeth had moved, rather than the town of Lawrence?

As the conductor moved from car to car announcing "Next stop, Bedford. Bedford is the next stop!" Jakes asked the man, "is Bedford in Lawrence County?"

"You bet it is. She's the county seat, and a prettier little town you won't find. Live there myself."

Jakes had one of his what-the-hell moments and got off the train in Bedford. He'd come this far; one more day wouldn't make a difference.

He asked for, and got, directions to the nearest place of lodging: a huge four-story structure named the Graystone Hotel. It was constructed, as were all the major buildings around the town's square, entirely of limestone. In the center of the square, the county court house and its grounds covered a complete block. Around it, but across a wide street, a bank, the post office, and a theater anchored three corners of the square. On the fourth corner loomed the Graystone Hotel.

Jamison Jakes had a plan, but not a new one now. He would find the local newspaper office and run an ad. The hotel clerk told Jakes the paper was the *Times-Mail* and it came out every Tuesday and Thursday, with a bigger edition on Sunday. Bedford was, after all, a center of commerce.

Before leaving for the *Times-Mail* office, Jakes did some editing to the ad on one of the *Lawrence Town Crier* copies he had stuck in this valise. The only major change he made was replacing "Pioneer Village" with "Graystone Hotel" and providing instructions for visitors to ask for Jamison Jakes at the desk. This meant he would be spending a great deal of time hanging out in the lobby; but he was determined not to be stuck in a room alone with a less than honorable person again. He also crossed out the reference regarding the egg lady.

On entering the newspaper office, Jakes was greeted warmly by a short man who was as big around as he was tall. His eyes sparkled in his rotund face and his smile seemed to reach ear to ear. "Well howdy, cowboy, what can I do for you?" The cowboy handle was one Jakes hadn't heard since leaving Omaha; he'd forgotten how much he missed it.

"I'd like to run a half-page ad in your paper if you have that kind of space and if I can get it in real soon."

"For a half-page we'll make the room! And as for real soon, how would day-after-tomorrow be?"

"You got yourself a deal."

"Alrighty-right! What do you want to put in the ad?"

"I'm lookin' to find a woman."

"Well, we've never been in the match-making business before, but for a half-page ad, I guess there's just about anything we'll do, so long as it's legal and wholesome."

"No, I'm not lookin' to find a woman for me." Jakes chuckled, "I'm lookin' to find a woman from another state who might've moved here some years ago."

The little cannonball laughed so hard at his mistaken assumption that his belly jiggled up and down.

As soon as the two quieted from their frivolity, Jamison Jakes unfolded the marked-up copy of the *Town Crier* ad and pulled out the tintype from his pocket. "Ran this up in the town of Lawrence a few days back. Didn't have any luck with it there."

The man looked at the ad, then held the tintype photograph close to his eyes, and squinted. Once again the ear-to-ear smile filled his face.

"Hell, buckaroo, I'd love to take your money, but you don't need to run an ad. This here is a picture of Elizabeth True. Must have been taken some time ago, but there's no doubt about it, that's Elizabeth. She teaches some of the upper grades down at the school. Everybody knows Elizabeth. She came up here from Tennessee right after her husband got killed in the war."

There it was. Just that simple. Be in the right place and things can be so easy.

Jakes stood still in a minor state of shock, but the next question brought him out of it.

"Why are you looking for Elizabeth?"

Oh, Lord! Thinking fast on his feet was not a Jamison Jakes talent unless his life was at stake, so he was surprised to hear his answer.

"I knew her husband in the war. We were in the same outfit. Just before he died, he gave me some things he wanted Elizabeth to have. And he asked me to give her a message. I got stuck out West after the war, and I'm just now gettin' back to these parts."

"Well, I know she'll be glad to get whatever you might have of her husband's. She surely did grieve over his loss. She came up here to get out of harm's way and have her baby in a safer place. Lived with a spinster aunt for awhile; when the old lady died, the town just took her under its wings."

Have her baby? Jakes did not ask.

"She never married again?" Jakes asked.

"Never did. Some folks thought it was because she kept some hope alive that he'd come back someday. She's made herself real busy learning how to be a teacher. She's been teaching for a number of years and the kids just love her. The parents do, too. Helps out at the Grace Methodist church quite a bit. She'd be doing more, I'm sure, except her boy needs a lot of looking after."

"Could you tell me how to find her?"

"Sure can. She lives in the last house at the end of F Street. All of our north-south streets follow the alphabet and the east-west streets have numbers. Right here, we're on the corner of Sixteenth and H, so you'll find the house without a problem."

"Hey, thanks. Can't tell you how much I appreciate gettin' this information."

"Any time, pard'ner. Glad I could help."

It was too late in the day for Jamison Jakes to find Elizabeth and still hope to have any time to talk. Tomorrow was Saturday, and Elizabeth wouldn't be teaching. If he arrived at her house mid-morning, he figured, their visit would be over in time for Jakes to still catch the afternoon train to New Albany.

The Graystone Hotel was classy. In addition to a large lobby with many overstuffed chairs placed alongside tables with inlaid-wood patterns, there was a large restaurant open from six in the morning until ten at night, a barroom with a man playing the piano, and even a barber shop. This time, Jakes conceded, he would get a shave and throw in a haircut, regardless of whether the barber was man or woman. He wanted to look presentable for morning.

He needed a workable strategy. What kind of tapestry should he weave in telling Elizabeth about Daniel True? He knew from talks with True that he and Elizabeth never married. Daniel hadn't mentioned having a son, so he obviously was unaware that Elizabeth was expecting a child when he left for the war. If Elizabeth had no husband when she arrived in Bedford, but was pregnant, then it would make sense for her to tell folks her husband was dead. She chose to use True as a married name, rather than using her maiden name when either would have sufficed with no one being the wiser, except for the spinster aunt who undoubtedly knew the real facts. Had the child not been True's, she surely would have picked another name.

Jakes decided he would gauge what he shared with Elizabeth as the discussion with her went along. If Daniel had been dead to her for all these years, maybe it would be best if he stay dead. One thing at least was becoming clear to Jakes: the father who lied to Elizabeth about Daniel True's being killed had also lied to True about Elizabeth's elopement.

Chapter 25

The walk along the residential streets of Bedford the following morning was pleasant. Large maple trees had finished dropping their leaves, and big piles of yellow and crimson were in most front yards waiting to be moved to the edge of the street and burned once the children tired of playing in them. Jamison Jakes noticed the center of the town was on a hilltop and going any direction away from the center meant going downhill, but the slope was very gradual and no one would have a problem walking back up.

Jakes found F Street without difficulty and headed south. He was in no hurry to get to his destination. Finding the right words to say when he talked with Elizabeth became very important with the additional information he had about her. He was never sure what Daniel True had meant when he said "tell Elizabeth." She needed to know Daniel was dead. But how should he have died? In the war, as she was told, but perhaps never believed? Some kind of illness? Indian attack? Being a hero in preventing a hotel robbery? Or as it really happened?

He reached the last house on the street, as much in a dilemma as when he'd set out from the hotel. He would just have to listen to whatever words came out of his mouth, hoping they would make sense.

With hat in hand, Jamison Jakes was at the threshold of the conclusion of his journey. He took a deep breath, held it, and rapped on the door.

After what seemed forever, a woman's voice from behind the closed door said, "Hello, who is it?"

"Name's Jamison Jakes, ma'am. I was a friend of your husband."

Total silence.

"Ma'am?"

No response.

"Ma'am, are you okay?"

"Yes. Please wait. I'll be with you in a minute."

Jakes felt his knees buckling, so he sat in the porch swing to keep from falling. He hadn't handled that well at all. Without even seeing her, he'd managed to shake the poor lady so badly she couldn't open the door.

After a couple of minutes, an eternity to Jamison Jakes, the door opened and Jakes jumped from the swing. There she was! The woman who had won and held the heart of Daniel True; the woman who had inspired a man to write letters knowing they couldn't be delivered; the woman who had lived inside the mind of his friend until the moment he died.

She was a woman of delicate beauty. Even though her blond hair was beginning to streak with gray, though her dress was simple and lacked color, she was a beautiful woman.

Looking at Jamison Jakes standing there on her porch, Elizabeth's eyes were a study of many emotions: disbelief, expectation, sorrow, and hope. Who was this man decked out in cowboy clothes? Why was he there, so many years after the war had ended? She expected she would have the answers soon, so she kept her emotions in check.

"Oh, I'm sorry, where are my manners?" Elizabeth said. "Please come inside. I'd like you to meet our son, Daniel. Come here, sweetie," she called, "we have company."

The young man who entered the room left no doubt that he was the son of Daniel True. The steel blue eyes, the long gangly legs, the square shoulders were Daniel True as he must have been so many years ago.

"Honey, this is Mister Jakes. He knew your father and he's come for a little visit. Will you tell Mister Jakes your name?"

The boy smiled and nodded his head. "My name is Daniel True and I live at 2131 F Street."

The words were understandable, but slurred. It was immediately obvious what the man at the newspaper office had meant when he said Elizabeth would be more involved in community activities if her son didn't require so much looking after. The morning was warm; Elizabeth told Daniel he could go play in the back yard.

She then turned her attention to her guest.

"You knew Daniel?"

"Yes, ma'am, I surely did."

"Were you with him in the war?"

Please Jesus, help me find the words, Jakes prayed silently. "No ma'am. We were both in the war, wearin' the gray, but we never met. We became friends just a short while back, out in Cheyenne."

There it was, out in the open. Jakes knew this wasn't a woman who deserved to hear any more hurtful lies.

Elizabeth's face showed both belief and disbelief. Her eyes began to well up with tears; her chin quivered.

"Then he wasn't killed in the war," she said hesitantly. "I never believed that he was. I knew he was still alive."

"Well, ma'am, that's the sad part. You see, he isn't alive any more. He was workin' for the law out in Colorado and was killed in the line of duty. With his dyin' breath, he asked me to find you."

"To tell me he is dead?"

"I suppose that's part of it, but I think mostly to tell you that he always loved you and that he thought about you every day. See, when he got back from the war, your pa told Daniel that you'd run off with your beau, got married, and moved up here to Indiana."

Tears continued streaming down her cheeks, but the sorrow etched on her face turned to anger and Jamison Jakes knew that she now realized what he had figured out the day before:

Elizabeth's father had fabricated stories about both Daniel and Elizabeth to keep them apart.

"That hypocrite!" she shouted. "How could he have done that to me? He had my mother and all of Daniel's friends believing Daniel was dead. He even put together a memorial service in the chapel of the college where they had taught so people could come and say nice things. And he spoke the nicest words of all. How could he have done that? How could he?"

Elizabeth sat for a long while staring out the window, watching young Daniel trying to skip rope. "At least I still have a part of him."

"Yes, ma'am. That boy's the spittin' image of his daddy."

"He has his father's looks, but not his mind. When I told my parents I was carrying a baby, they got me out of town real fast. My mother brought me up here to live with her sister and my father told me to never darken his door with my bastard child. I haven't seen either of them since. My aunt, however, was kindness itself. It was her idea that I take Daniel's name even though we weren't married. She carried that secret to her grave."

Jakes hesitated, and then asked, "What's wrong with the boy?"

"It happened when I was giving birth. I was so small and he was so big. It took more than a day for me to deliver. When he did come out, the cord was wrapped around his neck

189

and he was all blue and not breathing. It was winter and my aunt took the baby out into the yard and put him in a snow drift. The shock of the cold made him start crying. The doctor said that saved little Daniel's life, but his brain would never be what it should be."

In a way, Jakes was glad the subject had changed.

"Is there anything that can be done to make him better?"

"Yes, better. But he can never be cured. I've heard there's a new program up in Bloomington at Indiana College where they train people with problems like Daniel's to communicate more fully and to do simple problem-solving. They've also had some success teaching them to do jobs that will help them earn money."

"Can he get into that program?"

"Oh, I'm sure he could. But the program requires someone to stay there with the student for an entire year. It's a residential program but they don't provide supervision. And it's very expensive. I don't make much with my teaching job, just enough to make ends meet. I'd have to take a leave of absence if we went to Bloomington and there's just no way we could survive."

"Well, I hope something' can work out for the both of you. He's a fine lookin' boy, and I got a feelin' that there's a lotta jobs he could do with the proper trainin'."

Elizabeth gave no response, other than a slight nod. Jakes filled the silence.

"Ma'am, I gotta leave town this afternoon. Before I go, though, I got somethin' I want to give you that'll help you know what Daniel did with his life after leavin' Tennessee."

He hoped he could hand her the letters, say goodbye, and head back to the hotel before having to address the subject of how Daniel True had died. He reached inside his shirt and pulled out the bundle.

"These are letters Daniel wrote to you. There's one for every year since the war ended. You can tell I read some of 'em, and I want to say I'm sorry for that. I had no idea I'd ever see you and be givin' 'em to you."

The small woman took the letters in her hands and caressed them, put them against her cheek, then kissed them gently. She looked into Jamison Jakes' eyes and smiled with hers. "God bless you, Mister Jakes. Thank you for finding me to give me these. Daniel made a real friend when you came into his life."

Instinctively Jakes knew that Elizabeth needed to be alone with the letters, to read of Daniel True's love and devotion, his anger, and his frustration. She needed time alone with Daniel: her man, her lover...her husband.

To his surprise, Jakes found himself asking, "Could I maybe take young Daniel for a walk and get us a bite of lunch? I'd really like to get to know the boy better."

Elizabeth's tightened lips didn't move, but she nodded a thankful approval.

Jamison Jakes and young Daniel True strolled slowly toward the center of town. It was still well before noon and there was no rush to get the boy home. He was easy to be with, walking stride by stride with Jakes. Many passersby greeted Daniel by name; Daniel nodding and smiling in return.

The two went by the Monon station so Jakes could recheck the departure of the afternoon train and to make sure his ticket to New Albany was valid since his stopover in Bedford hadn't been arranged in advance. The ticket was approved to use for the rest of the trip. There was a celebration being held on the platform, which must have had to do with something significant regarding the railroad's history. School girls wearing bib overalls and train engineer hats were singing,

> *All up and down the Monon,*
> *Everything is fine.*
> *On that rootin'-tootin' Monon,*

It's the Hoosier Line.

Daniel pretended to be the choir director, much to the delight of the small crowd. Before continuing their walk, they helped themselves to cake that was being handed out by a couple of women.

They had lunch at a café near a corner of the square then went to the Graystone Hotel so Jakes could pack his valise for the afternoon trip south. It was then he noticed that the envelopes marked One, Two, and Three hadn't been included with the letter packet. He started to put them inside his shirt, to take along to Elizabeth, but thought better of that idea. The first poem, composed by Daniel True on some battlefield, was intended for Elizabeth to read. But the second one was from True to himself, and so mournfully sad, that it shouldn't be given to Elizabeth. He decided quickly to give her only the first poem.

Chapter 26

Elizabeth was sitting on the porch swing, a shawl around her shoulders, when Jamison Jakes and young Daniel returned to the house. She smiled when she saw them and placed the letters, which she had been holding close to her chest, onto her lap. Daniel headed for the backyard to play and Jakes took a seat in a rocking chair a few feet away from the swing. Neither spoke. He knew that her thoughts were in another place. He would wait for her to return.

Looking at her, Jakes tried to imagine what her life would be like at this point had there been no war, or at least no deception by her father. Although she had been alone with her son for so many years, she had kept her beauty, her poise and – most of all – her courage. He had known only one other woman to be her equal. Daniel True's love of, and devotion to, this woman was certainly understandable.

"He was a good man," Elizabeth said softly. "A good, wonderful man."

"That's for sure, ma'am."

Another few minutes of silence passed before she spoke again. "It means so much to me that he had you for a friend. Not many men would do what you've done. I can be at peace now. Even though it's a sad peace, it's so much better than not knowing. These letters will be my warmth in the winter and my cool breeze in the summer. I feel like I'm at a new beginning and can start looking ahead now, instead of living in the past."

"Elizabeth." Jakes' felt tightness in his chest. This was the first time he had spoken her name. "Elizabeth, there's somethin' else your husband wanted you to have. I got it here for you."

Jakes reached inside his shirt and pulled out the envelope marked with the "One" and handed it to her. She reached inside and pulled out the contents. There was the poem -- and a stack of one-hundred dollar bills.

"What is this?" Elizabeth wasn't at all sure what to make of this considerable amount of money. She was puzzled.

"It's reward money that Daniel earned when he captured a man called the Widowmaker. That hombre was the meanest cuss that was ever was born and Daniel made up his mind that he was gonna stop him from ever killin' again. So him and me tracked the Widowmaker for days in the snow and when we caught up with him, there was a showdown."

"Is that when Daniel was killed?"

"Yes. We could've a put a slug in him from an ambush, but that wasn't the way Daniel worked. He kept sayin' his job was to catch 'em and somebody else's job to prove their guilt. So he went into the clearin' where the Widowmaker was and tried to arrest him. He had the drop on the skunk and made him toss his pistol, but the snake had another one hidden in his bedroll, and when he picked the roll up to tie it to his horse, he pulled out the gun and shot Daniel. But Daniel got him, too."

Elizabeth was lost in thought, absolutely quiet, then asked,

"Did Daniel die immediately?"

"No, he lived for a minute or two. That's when he said to me, 'Find Elizabeth and tell her how much I love her.' His last thought was about you. Then he went on to heaven."

"What about this money?"

"There was a reward of five-thousand dollars on the Widowmaker's head put up by a citizens group in Cheyenne. After I gave Daniel a real good buryin', I hauled the Widowmaker into town and they gave me the reward money. I knew it wasn't mine though, so I've been keepin' it to give to you once I found you."

Elizabeth set the money aside to read the poem and once again the tears began to flow.

"I hope there's enough money for you to get young Daniel into that program up in Bloomington," Jakes said.

"Yes! Oh yes! I know this will be enough. Maybe even more than enough."

When it was time to leave the house and make for the train station, Elizabeth asked if she and Daniel could walk along. Jakes knew a lot about Daniel True, and it was important to Elizabeth that she share some things about herself. She started by telling of her childhood in Tennessee, the happy times and the sad; of when she met Daniel for the first time when she was a child; of the little things he would do for her that showed her she was special; of hoping that he would wait for her to grow up; of notes he would slip to her in church; of falling in love; of becoming lovers the night before he was to leave for war.

As they strolled along Jamison Jakes found himself thinking this must be what having a family is like: taking walks together, talking, laughing, greeting neighbors. He felt sorry that his friend never had the experience of spending time with his wife and son.

The three stopped by the Graystone Hotel for Jakes to pick up his valise and arrived at the train station with a few minutes to spare.   Before he boarded the train for his trip to New Albany and then on the Lexington, Elizabeth took both of Jamison Jakes' hands in hers and held them tightly.

"God bless you and keep you safe. Be happy and well. I'll never forget what you have done for us." She stood on tiptoes and kissed his cheek.

Jakes then turned and shook the hand of young Daniel. "Happy and well," the boy said.

On the train, Jakes went to the rear platform and watched as a waving Elizabeth True and her son disappeared from sight.

Chapter 27

Jamison Jakes' mind, while working hard to sort through all that had happened over the past six hours, was more at ease than he could ever remember. He was, at the same time, exhilarated and exhausted. In the short while he had spent with Elizabeth and young Daniel, he had witnessed strength, fragility, commitment, hope dashed, hope regained, and love – love that was so deep, so steadfast, it was beyond Jakes' ability to fully grasp.

While the two never spoke of the contents of the letters Jakes hadn't read, he knew by Elizabeth's demeanor that they were special. She would have this part of Daniel True forever. His words would be her solace. She could read and reread the letters time and again while picturing him, sitting at a table or standing at a bar, thinking only of her as he wrote.

Jakes smiled with self-satisfaction at the way he told the story of the Daniel True –Widowmaker showdown. That was a simple, heroic way for Daniel to have died, and left the

Alamo Kid out of it.

The sixty mile trip from Bedford to New Albany meant he would arrive after dark. With so much on his mind at the Bedford station he hadn't thought to check the schedule of service between New Albany and Louisville, leaving his night uncertain. If this night was the only uncertainty facing him, his future would be clearer. In giving the five-thousand dollars to Elizabeth, Jakes no longer had the bankroll to buy a small farm or a general store. Once again he found himself with limited options.

If Jamison Jakes had one talent, it was how to survive, but in the short time he had spent with Elizabeth, he knew now he wanted more from life than just staying alive. Daniel True had been a survivor who had experienced a lifetime of love with little more than memories to sustain him. Jakes' life was more forgettable than memorable.

Except for Maryalice. While he and Elizabeth and young Daniel were walking to the train station, Jakes had experienced flashes of Maryalice in the place of Elizabeth. For one brief moment, he almost took Elizabeth's hand in his, stopping short of actually doing so when he realized who she was.

Jakes needed a cup of coffee. He opened his valise to dig for his coffee cup and to go to the café car. Before finding the cup, he came across the two envelopes he hadn't given to Elizabeth: those marked "Two" and "Three." The coffee could wait. He wanted to read the third message. He carefully opened the envelope.

At the top of the sheet, as with the other two, Daniel True had made a note as to where he was at the time of the writing. This one said, "At the relay station between Denver and Cheyenne." Jamison Jakes' heart raced. This had been written at Pappy's shack before Jakes' had caught up with Daniel, just two days before the bounty hunter died. It was a poem titled "Thoughts on the Wind."

The ebony clouds are gathering.

They have been since I first saw the sun.
Small then, and unthreatening. And I smiled
for they seemed so far away.
"So what if they do come?" I reasoned
with unclear mind.
"I have been in storms before,
Storms that cut to heart's core,
Storms that beat to soul's dismay,
Storms that carry hope away,
Storms that with banshee threat
Beat and pound and make stones sweat...
Yes, I have been in storms before."

But that was when the clouds were small,
Before the wind began to call, "Elizabeth,
Elizabeth."
Hear it now? Great God! the wind talks.
What will the world think with the wind
calling "Elizabeth."

Dark clouds laughing, crying shame;
Strong men laughing, limping lame;
Women crying in the streets;
Children eating Christmas treats;
Old men sleeping in the grass;
Angels playing horns of brass;
Birds eating snails from bottomless pails.
Remorseful tears – congenital fears.
I cry.

And I die! Although I breathe and walk and stare,
I am as dead as if a savage's arrow has
pierced my heart!

Being dead, I am in Hell. And Hell is

> *listening to the wind calling "Elizabeth,*
> *Elizabeth!"*
> *And knowing I will never see her again.*

Jamison Jakes sat looking at the words, the last Daniel True would ever write, and his entire body seemed numb. He'd never known it was possible to have such feelings, but now he was in the grip of emotions that, while sad, made him realize that every life has meaning, that people do need people who matter to them, that love and devotion are as important as food and water.

He was so lost in thought that before he knew it, the train was pulling into the New Albany depot. He put the poem and his coffee cup back in the valise, entered the station, sat heavily on a bench, and stared at the floor.

There were only a few people milling around, and the loudest sound was coming from the dots and dashes of a telegraph key. Jamison Jakes got up and moved slowly toward the sound, picked up a "Message to be Sent" form, and began filling it in.

TO: Maryalice Wheeler
Nugget Inn
Denver Colorado

MESSAGE: Dear Maryalice. I am coming home. I hope you will be looking for me

FROM: Jamison Jakes

He handed the form to the telegrapher who counted the words and collected the amount due. The message would reach Denver by morning.

Jakes returned to the bench that would be his bed for the night. Reaching into the valise, he pulled out his book and turned to Part Two of *The Pilgrim's Progress.*

CPSIA information can be obtained
at www.ICGtesting.com
Printed in the USA
FFHW020841131218
49866293-54435FF

9 781598 009521